# Aisle Kill Him

## Felicity Philips Investigates

## Book 3

### Steve Higgs

'Aisle Kill Him' is a work of fiction. Names, characters, businesses, organisations, places, events and incidents either are the product of the author's imagination or are used fictitiously. Any resemblance to actual persons, living or dead, events or locations is entirely coincidental.

## Dedication

To Nora Morley, my maternal grandmother.

**Table of Contents**

Kill the Competition

Deploy the Spies

The Difference Between a Cat and a Dog

Mad Skillz

Backed into a Corner

Criminal Behaviour

Millennials and Inches

Puppy Training

Winning the Battle

Fruitless Search

What Heroes Do

A Clue Not Seen

First Date Jitters

Confrontation

What Heroes Do Part Two

Best to Keep Quiet When Concussed

Pets to the Rescue

Sneak Attack

How Devious is a Cat?

Coffee Shop Chatter

Animal Behaviour

The Truth

Gremlins?

Fat Badger

Exchanging Insults

New Employee

Killer in our Midst

Zombiez!

When is a Crime Scene not a Crime Scene?

Danger Never Sleeps

Probably Should have Told Her

Not What I Thought

Figuring it Out

Catching Fish

Epilogue – Four Days After the Wedding Fayre

Author Notes

What's Next for Felicity

A FREE Rex and Albert Story

Free Amber and Buster story

More Cozy Mystery by Steve Higgs

Blue Moon Investigations

More Books by Steve Higgs

Free Books and More

I just couldn't get the flowers to sit right. It was taking me all the way back to being in the Brownies and being made to sit my flower arranging badge. I hadn't liked going to Brownies every week. I didn't like the uniform or the hat I had to wear which made my scalp itch like I had a lice infestation.

That was all way behind me now in the distant past, but this was taking me right back — I just couldn't get the flowers to sit right.

'Here, Mrs Philips, let me,' offered Jessica in her delightful Irish accent. 'Me ma owned a florist shop and made me work there every day until I was old enough to decide what I wanted to do. '

Irritated by the inanimate objects, I bit my lip and stepped back to let the young redhead tackle the task.

Eight seconds later, the flower arrangement looked perfect.

I muttered a word my local vicar would not have approved of and smiled sweetly at Jessica when she turned to check my opinion.

'I think ma expected me to stay on in the shop,' she explained, 'but I was fed up picking rose thorns out of my fingertips by then, and I really wanted to be in the beauty industry.'

Jessica isn't someone I know. I'd only met her two minutes ago when Mindy spotted the hairdresser loitering by our stand and asked her a question about a new style she was considering.

'Very well done, Jessica,' I congratulated her though I secretly wanted to accidentally knock the flower water onto the seat of her chair just as she was about to sit down. Not that I would ever do anything so petty and childish. Goodness, no. Not me.

1

You see, my name is Felicity Philips, and I am the top wedding planner in the county. In truth, I would consider myself among the top in the country and had a plan to make sure everyone else soon thought the same.

The plan involved a certain prince and his intention to marry a young lady called Nora Morley. The chance to helm a royal wedding was the sort of opportunity that came along once or maybe twice in a generation. It was as rare as hen's teeth. And I had manoeuvred myself into the frame to be considered. Now all I needed was a clear run of successful weddings.

Yeah, that wasn't exactly going to plan.

There had been a couple of deaths recently, and by deaths I mean grisly murders. Not that any of the deaths were my fault, I was just the wedding planner helming the events at which the deaths occurred. Nevertheless, I could not help worrying that were the trend to continue, no one would want to hire me. I would become a pariah in the wedding world, shunned by client and partner firm alike.

Today was a new day though. My team and I were in a glitzy London hotel for one of the country's most prestigious wedding fayres and we were going to shine.

'Ah, Flicky. Couldn't quite afford one of the best spots, eh?' brayed a voice from behind me.

I felt my muscles tense at the sound of her voice. It was an undesirable yet automatic reaction. As I forced them to ease, I set my face to its most engaging mode and twisted around on my heels to face my arch-nemesis.

Primrose Green is everything that I am not. She is tall, she is twenty years younger than me and glamourous, plus she is unfairly attractive and has the children I never managed to achieve. She is one of the other top wedding planners in the county and a contender for the royal wedding.

'Hello, Primrose.' I smiled up at her while imagining jamming a raw chicken leg into her mouth. 'Thankfully, Melissa,' the event coordinator and hotel deputy manager, 'called me before she opened the event to anyone else and offered me my choice of spots. She knows I am too savvy to be conned into paying the stupid price they want for a stall in the centre ring.' Where Primrose had hers. 'Plus, knowing this business as well as I do, I knew I would ambush ninety percent of the customers visiting this event long before they got to you.'

My smile was genuine now, mostly because Primrose's had frozen in place. She was fighting to keep it there, but she couldn't fake the emotion behind her eyes.

We are both at the top of our game. However, while I am there because I work hard and attract top celebrity and super-rich clients because I know what I am doing, Primrose is fireworks, clever marketing, and sparkly lights to lure the unsuspecting client.

Kind of like one of those deep-sea fish with the light thingy that hangs off its head. A deep-sea angler fish. That's it! The ones with the huge mouths. Primrose is a deep-sea angler fish. Get too close and she will pounce and eat you.

Unable to dredge up a worthwhile response, Primrose shifted her attention to pick holes in my booth and my presentation. She was going to find something unpleasant to say, but found herself utterly disarmed when I dismissed her to talk to a young couple arriving at the front entrance of my booth.

I heard what she said next, but happily acted as if I hadn't as I joined Mindy in greeting our next potential opportunity. Jessica was no longer with my niece, undoubtedly returning to her firm's stand wherever that was.

My booth had several different customers in and around it. One couple, rich rather than famous, were sitting at a table with Justin Metcalf, my master of ceremonies. He is a lean man who dresses elegantly, if a little flamboyantly. He is married with children and a steady rock who has been at my side for many years.

We were all here to sell our product – the best weddings you can get, and if history were to repeat itself from the previous few years, we would walk away with over a million pounds worth of new wedding orders spread over the coming months and years.

Somewhere behind me, Primrose still hadn't gone back to her own booth. I wanted to kick her out but couldn't see an easy way to do that. Mindy, my assistant and also my niece, is a karate expert and could remove my rival by force quite easily. However, that is not the done thing and would be frowned upon by the event organisers. This is the biggest wedding exhibition event of the year, and I could not risk getting banned for starting a fight.

I glanced over my shoulder to find Primrose looking at my brochures. As I squinted in her direction, my eyes narrowing with suspicion, she must have felt me looking because she twitched her head to catch me glaring at her.

Was she thinking about stealing all my brochures, so I had none to hand out? I would not put it past her.

I was just thinking that I ought to politely ask her to leave when I spotted Melissa Cartwright, the Hotel deputy manager and coordinator for this event. She was just passing the back of my booth, undoubtedly coming from one of the behind-the-scenes areas.

'Melissa!' I called, raising my arm to wave so she would see where the shout had come from. But my voice must have been drowned out by the background chatter because she carried on her merry way.

Mindy was leading the couple we had been talking to across the booth to another table where we would get a little more in depth into what their dream wedding entailed. I needed to join her but chose to spend just a couple of minutes making sure I engaged with the other potential clients investigating my displays. I would also politely ask Primrose to return to her own area, but when I looked, she was already gone, weaving through the crowd and easy to spot because she is taller in her heels than half of the men.

With a deep breath, I let my smile form as nature intended and set off to schmooze the lovely couples looking to tie their particular knot in a thoroughly expensive and exclusive manner.

I got half a step.

The scream of sheer horror from the young woman directly to my front shot through me like an icy lance to my heart.

Her betrothed was holding onto one of the steel columns of my booth and twitching spasmodically. Almost dancing on the spot, there was clearly something affecting him. Champagne from the complimentary glass he held was jumping and sploshing to land on the floor.

A half second had passed. The woman was still screaming, and her right hand was coming up to grab her boyfriend/fiancée.

My feet were just starting to move again, my reaction automatic, no thought being applied. The man was in dire trouble, and I needed to try to help him.

As if watching in slow motion, I could see Mindy leaping to her feet. She was as far away as she could be while still inside our booth, but I knew how fast she was.

Justin was also getting to his feet, worry gripping his features as he raced to give aid.

One of the venue's security men – my brain idly supplied that it was the head of security I met earlier – was outside the booth but rushing to help as well. A water bottle, one of those sports ones, flew from his hand as he burst into motion. He was going to get there first, the simple speed/time/distance calculation performed by my brain as I lunged for the poor man.

The head of security – I could not remember his name – screamed at the girlfriend/fiancé as she tried to grab her intended.

'No!' he roared.

I expected him to grab the stricken man who was still twitching as if his body were connected to the mains, but instead he slammed into the woman, bearing her to the ground and then pulling her away.

I was less than a yard from the man and committed to grabbing him myself now. With my hand reaching forward, it was only then that my own thoughts caught up to me.

'Auntie, no!' yelled Mindy from somewhere behind me.

The man was twitching as if connected to the mains because that was exactly what I was seeing. He was being electrocuted before my eyes and I was about to touch him, completing a circuit that would see me endure the same deadly torment.

Could I even change my trajectory now?

The answer was no. I was moving too fast and had gotten far too close. Even if I whipped my arms away, I would run into him before I could change my course.

And that is exactly what I did.

Knowing what was about to happen, I closed my eyes and gritted my teeth. Perhaps I would bounce off him and get away with nothing worse than a nasty shock.

Trying to aim myself so that my collision would be a glancing blow that might send me clear, I nevertheless hit him square on. I might not weigh much, I am rather petite, but I had enough force to knock him over. We were going down and I was going to land on top of him.

It was about as bad as it could be.

But as my brain screamed in terror, I realised nothing else was happening. I wasn't being electrocuted. I wasn't being … anything.

We slammed into the carpeted floor of my booth with the man on his back and me lying on his chest. I rolled over and away in an instant and just as a dozen more people arrived.

Sitting on the floor, my breaths coming in savage gulps, I saw the head of security kneel to check the victim's pulse.

The sorrowful shake of his head preceded a fresh wail from the man's betrothed.

Whoever the man was, he was dead.

He died in my booth.

And Primrose Green killed him.

The head of security, and a visitor to the event who turned out to be a medical professional, did their best performing CPR, but the man was beyond saving.

At the same time, a swift investigation revealed a damaged cable running to our refrigerator. We were using it to keep our champagne and other drinks cold. Unseen by anyone at the back of our booth where we bordered the edge of the event, it was touching the structure of the booth itself. The whole frame of our booth was live and might have been for some time.

It went unnoticed until someone touched it. That poor person was Douglas Irwin, a potential client until a few moments ago. I only escaped being electrocuted because the circuit overloaded and tripped out the breakers just as I collided with him.

The poor man, pronounced dead and covered with Justin's jacket, was twenty-seven and the owner of an online marketing firm.

Douglas was the unlucky one who touched the frame first. It could have been anyone.

I felt terrible, but I also felt rage. The cable hadn't been damaged when we set up this morning. I quizzed Justin and Mindy and they agreed. The refrigerator was new bought specifically for this event and while I acknowledged that the crew who put up our booth could have accidentally cut through the cable's outer sheath, I was having a hard time believing it. The timing was just too perfect.

'That is a dangerous thing to accuse anyone of without proof,' warned Justin.

There was a crowd around our booth, but it was mostly security now and event management. Melissa had been informed of the tragedy and was back to supervise the situation. Under her guidance, screens were arriving to close our area off. We were done for the day, that much was obvious.

We could get out among the crowd and hand out leaflets and brochures, make the best of what we had and score some new clients anyway. However, I wanted to focus my efforts on proving Douglas Irwin's death was no accident.

'Primrose was here right before it happened,' I pointed out for the third or fourth time. 'She knows I will beat her to the royal wedding gig, and she is going to do everything she can to stop that from happening. I never thought she would go this far.'

'Auntie, you don't really think she did it on purpose, do you?'

I shot my niece a questioning look. 'Cut the wire? Yes. Murder someone … that was probably not her intention, but I honestly would not put it past her. It's more likely she wanted to kill me.'

'There are better ways to kill a person,' Justin argued. 'If your demise was her intention, she had no way of knowing who would touch the frame first.'

'That's right,' I shot back, surprising my master of ceremonies by agreeing with him. 'I think it didn't matter who the victim was. On top of the recent run of bad luck we have suffered, she would be betting on this to be a last straw for anyone looking to hire me. She's probably on the phone now calling the editor of *Weddings* magazine. If she can discredit me, she will do.'

Mindy tried to calm me down a little. 'Okay, Auntie. Let's assume Primrose did this. How do we prove it?'

It was a great question. It was also an annoying one because I didn't have an answer. In the last few weeks, I had unwittingly solved three cases. I say unwittingly because I didn't really solve them at all. It would be more accurate to say that I ran around screaming in terror half the time and stumbled across the truth by accident.

Or, I could say that my cat and dog helped me identify the killer in each case. I have a rather unique skill that I will claim I was born with – I can talk to my cat and dog. Just those two, no others, and it only started after they had been living with me for a while.

I haven't worked out the why or the how of it yet. I can hear their voices in my head, and like all animals they understand humans when we speak. If you are now questioning how much your own cat or dog understands, the likely answer is everything. However, as if it were agreed many millennia ago, they choose to pretend they have no idea what our funny noises mean.

Unless we say something they want to hear, that is. You can test this yourself. Go into a room your dog is not in and say at a normal conversation volume it is time to go to the vet. I bet you get no response. Now quietly ask if they would like a biscuit and count how many nanoseconds it takes for them to arrive, skidding to a halt, at your feet.

Buster, my Bulldog, will do anything I ask and likes to pretend he is a superhero called Devil Dog. I genuinely believe he means it when he asks me to buy him a cape and a mask to hide his identity. In contrast, my pedigree Ragdoll cat, Amber, is more mercenary. I can get her to do what I need, but there is generally a negotiation first.

11

They were upstairs in my suite where they were hopefully not trying to kill each other. I could employ them both to help me listen in on Primrose's conversations. I was going to trick her into revealing the truth so I could clear any blame coming my way and send her to jail where she belonged.

Yeah. That's what I was going to do!

'How about the private detective you know?' asked Justin.

'Vince?' Mindy supplied his name. 'Yeah, he would drop whatever he might be doing to help out for sure.'

'No!' I snapped far more harshly and quickly than I intended. Trying again, I aimed for calm and thoughtful. 'No, he will have work of his own, Mindy. We should leave him to get on with it and attend to this ourselves.'

Justin wasn't used to hearing me snap at anyone and was giving me a surprised look.

Mindy caught his eye. 'Vince gets Aunt Felicity hot under the collar. She keeps claiming they are not involved but they seem to keep ending up naked together.'

Mindy had been annoying me about this for weeks now and I was giving serious consideration to firing her.

'He does not get me hot anywhere, thank you,' I almost snarled.

Mindy just chuckled and backed away a pace, feigning a need to get out of striking range.

Any further discussion of the subject was curtailed by the arrival of Melissa, the event manager.

'Mrs Philips,' Melissa spoke my name to make sure she had my attention. 'How are you feeling?'

I met her with a grim expression. Rightly so given the circumstances.

Justin, standing just behind me now that we had swivelled around to speak to Melissa, leaned in close to my head so he could whisper.

'Don't tell her you suspect Primrose Green, Felicity.'

It was an unnecessary warning. Accusing my rival and getting the hotel management involved would achieve nothing. It was more likely to make me look crazy. They were all looking at the damaged cable as a terrible and tragic accident. There was nothing to suggest foul play even if I knew better.

Clearing my throat with a small cough, I said, 'I do not intend to reopen my booth, Melissa. Doing so would be unseemly.' Besides, the coroners would arrive soon to take Mr Irwin away and going back in directly after would make me feel squeamish.

Melissa inclined her head, agreeing with me but doing so as she acknowledged how hard that was for me and my business.

'Perhaps you could reopen tomorrow?' she suggested. 'We can leave the barriers up until tonight and take them down for you to reset. If you want to,' she added. 'There are still two days of the event left.'

She was right about that. Set to run Friday through to Sunday, we were barely halfway into the first day. Also, if I folded my booth now, would I still be able to justify hanging around and snooping on Primrose for the rest of the weekend?

I nodded thoughtfully. 'Thank you, Melissa. I will take some time to absorb what has happened but will probably do as you suggest.'

She reached out to touch my arm, imparting her support. 'This is a terrible accident, but you should not blame yourself. We should be glad Reed was so close by. As I understand it, his swift reactions prevented anyone else from being hurt.'

'Reed?' I questioned. 'Is that the head of security?'

'Yes,' Melissa confirmed.

I had already thanked him, of course. His swift reactions saved Douglas' fiancée from probable death and certain injury. That he was so close by was serendipitous indeed.

'I'm afraid I must go, Mrs Philips,' Melissa backed away a pace. 'This … situation,' she chose her word carefully, 'requires careful management. If you need anything at all, please just let me know.' She bowed her head in goodbye as she made to spin around and walk away but paused for one last comment. 'I do hope you will stay for the rest of the weekend, Mrs Philips. Please do not feel obligated though. This event will always welcome you back, no matter what you decide to do.'

I dipped my head in a show of thanks and watched her return to the security team on the other side of my booth.

Still feeling terrible about what had happened, though not even slightly guilty because I hadn't done it, I sucked in a deep breath to steady myself.

'What's next, Auntie?' Mindy wanted to know.

With a resolute firmness to my tone, I replied, 'It's time to deploy my spies.'

*'What nonsense are you watching?'* asked Amber. The Ragdoll cat stretched out her front paws and arched her back. Until a few seconds ago she had been fast asleep on the bed and content the dog could not easily disturb her. She awoke when an explosion on the television tore through her slumbering state.

Buster liked to watch television - cops shows and action-adventure films especially. Felicity knew this and was generally good enough to leave the television on when she went out. Focused on the car chase playing out before his eyes, Buster heard the cat speak but saw no reason to respond.

Squinting at the screen, Amber could make no sense of what she could see. It was just humans running around and doing violent things. It all looked like a lot of effort when there was perfectly good sleeping as an alternative.

Nevertheless, she didn't like being ignored and would never let the dog think he had the upper hand.

*'Hey, mannerless oaf,'* she hissed at him from her lofty position. *'Hey, your mother was a mongrel and used to get friendly with badgers in alleyways.'*

Buster was used to the constant abuse from the cat yet despite that could not find a way to ignore her for any length of time.

Tensing his muscles for a speedy attack, he threw himself backward and around to fly at the cat. In his head, it was just like Neo in *The Matrix*, the camera forced to track around the entire room just to keep up with the speed of his movement.

In reality, he was about as speedy as a sloth eating toffee.

He charged the side of the bed, jumping at it but misjudging his timing so he leapt too early and came crashing down into the side of the bed frame with his head.

The bed shunted a foot sideways.

Shaking his head to clear it, Buster looked up at the cat. He couldn't get on the bed to chase her and exact retribution for her insults, his body just wasn't designed for jumping onto things. He couldn't really do anything except vow revenge which was what he did.

Using mostly words which could never be printed.

Amber stared down at him with her giant blue eyes. '*Wow. There were some inventive terms that time. Well done, Buster.*'

'*Bite me,*' he snapped back.

Amber pulled a face. '*Ewwww. No thanks. I might catch something terrible.*'

I didn't know anything about their conversation, of course, nor could I tell that further intellectual debate got cut short when I entered the room.

I gave myself a moment to inspect the room for damage. The bed appeared to have moved but otherwise there was nothing to indicate my pets had been fighting.

Buster arrived at my feet, wagging his stumpy tail madly and trying not to pee in his excitement.

'I hope you two have been getting along,' I chided, dropping the room key back in my handbag.

16

'*Don't be ridiculous,*' scoffed Amber, flicking her tail idly.

I sat on the edge of the bed to stroke her fur, the cat obliging by allowing me to do so.

'Now then, Amber, Buster is a sweet dog and the two of you have got into and out of scrapes together. I think you like each other far more than you let on.'

Amber cracked one eye to glare at me. '*I would sooner live with a hippo.*'

Buster echoed her sentiment. '*I would rather dye my fur pink and hang out on street corners turning tricks for gay Dobermans than live with that cat.*'

That was quite the picture.

Mindy came into my room and closed the door.

'What were you doing?' I asked, wondering why she had been hanging around in the corridor outside.

She wiggled her phone at me. 'I'm a teenager, I was tweeting my status.'

Thinking nothing more of it, I got down to business.

'Buster, Amber, Felicity needs your help.'

'*Devil Dog reporting for duty!*' trumpeted Buster as he galloped across the carpet from greeting Mindy to arrive by my feet.

'*What's in it for me?*' asked Amber, my pets demonstrating the fundamental difference between cats and dogs in just two sentences.

'What are they saying?' asked Mindy.

17

I looked away from Buster's eager expression to meet Mindy's questioning gaze. Mindy knows I can communicate with my pets; she was bright enough to work it out. Or, more accurately, I am not very good at having conversations with my pets and keeping it so no one will notice what I am doing.

Vince knows too.

Solving those cases I mentioned earlier required the intimate help of my pets and I couldn't manage to do that without those closest to me seeing what I was doing.

'Buster wants to help,' I explained. Buster wagged his tail even harder. 'Amber wants to negotiate remuneration.'

'*That's because I am not a drooling moron,*' replied Amber calmly. '*Plus, my assistance in whatever matter you wish to engage me, is worth something. I have skills.*'

'*So do I,*' insisted Buster.

'*If we include loud belching, breath that can strip paint, ramming things with your head and generally acting like an imbecile, then yes, Buster, you are highly skilled.*'

Buster lunged for the bed again, this time getting his front paws up so his head was at the same height as the cat's paws.

He snarled and barked in his frustrated anger.

Amber batted his nose with a paw. '*Go away. Or I shall do it again with my claws out.*'

I pulled Amber away and pushed Buster down with a gentle foot.

'That's enough, both of you.'

Buster narrowed his eyes at Amber. *'One day I am going to catch you asleep somewhere, cat. When I do, I'm going to whoopee cushion you.'*

When Amber and I both stared at him, he expanded to explain.

*'Sit on you and make fart noises. I won't be using my mouth to make the sounds,'* he added in case any clarity was needed. It wasn't.

As I screwed up my face in disgust, Amber shot me a told-you-so look. *'You see what I have to put up with. Look, we are already in London. Battersea Dogs' Home isn't that far from here. Let's just drop him off there and make him someone else's problem. They still euthanise there, don't they?'*

I scooped Amber under my arm and stood up.

'Listen, the pair of you. Felicity is in trouble. That means we are in trouble. You two are going to work together and help me or there will be no chewy marrowbone treats,' I met Buster's eyes. 'And there will be no poached mackerel,' I turned my not-to-be-argued-with expression on Amber.

Huffing loudly, Amber looked down at the dog.

*'Truce,'* she enquired, showing her maturity, and extending an olive branch.

Buster thought for a second before making his decision. *'Cat, you can get stuffed.'*

After I gave him a good talking to, Mindy took Buster's lead and he trotted merrily along the corridor to the elevators. It was another major difference between cats and dogs. Buster, like most dogs, was almost perpetually happy. Even when I was telling him off, he smiled and wagged his tail. Now that we were going somewhere, the whole incident was behind him and forgotten.

Amber, by contrast, was seething with pent up rage and was going to extract revenge on the dog at some point regardless of what I said or did.

Inside I was sighing because I needed their help.

'What is Justin up to?' Mindy asked as the elevator car travelled silently down to the ground floor.

'I told him to go home. He was travelling home each night anyway, he might as well take advantage of us having to shut early today.'

Mindy had nothing else to say until the doors swished open once more, spilling us into the plush hotel lobby. The Randecaux had been standing on the same site for over a hundred and fifty years and, according to them, its doors had never closed. Boasting over three hundred rooms in the centre of London and not far from Victoria Station and Buckingham Palace, I knew to book well in advance because the hotel, and the wedding fayre they hosted, was a hot ticket.

People with money who wanted to find all their wedding solutions under one roof came here. Celebrities, sports stars, the newly rich with money burning a hole in their pocket, plus older men trying to impress their much younger soon-to-be third wife, or vice versa in some cases with rich women snagging a younger man, all lined up to spend more than was needed on a single day.

Through a set of double doors in the hotel lobby, one could access the Randecaux's event hall. They hosted other events throughout the year, tailoring the hall to meet different needs. At the wedding fayre, visitors would find wedding dress designers, makeup artists, and hairdressers, all of whom were at the top of their game and could invent a price for the services on the spot and yet still get paid. There were horse drawn carriages and horses, harpists and string quartets, firms selling alternative weddings where the bridal party might all wish to skydive while the vows are read. Or maybe shark cage weddings were the flavour this year. That is firmly not my end of the wedding market.

'Ooh, Lipizzaners,' cooed Mindy as a parade of four beautiful white horses trotted through the centre of the exhibition.

'*Wow!*' woofed Buster. '*Now those are big dogs.*'

'*They are horses, you moron,*' purred Amber, reclining in my arms as if she deserved to be carried everywhere.

'*Okay,*' Buster wagged his tail uncertainly. '*What sort of dog is a horse?*'

I chose to let the question go unanswered because Amber was suddenly alert.

'*Hold the phone,*' she murmured excitedly.

I had to grab her quickly or she would have been on the floor and running.

'Leave the swans alone,' I insisted. 'They will chew you up and spit you out, you silly cat.'

'*It's just a big white duck,*' she sneered. '*Since when was a bird ever a challenge for a cat?*'

21

'*Since there were pterodactyls?*' offered Buster.

Amber ignored him. '*Bringing one of those down would put a fine cap on my day. What do they taste of?*'

'Evil vengeance,' I assured her.

'*Ha!*' snorted Amber. '*I shall smite them and eat them!*'

'What, all of them?' I whispered into the fur at the base of her neck so it wasn't too obvious I was talking to my cat. 'Each of them is five times your size.'

There were doves too, though the smaller white birds were in a large cage. I knew the man responsible for the birds. He owned a large plot of land outside Canterbury in Kent and specialised in training his swans and other birds to behave among crowds of people. The swans were all hand reared. He called the business Feathered Guests and did rather well for himself by charging a sum so ludicrous it made the service utterly exclusive. Somehow that made it more desirable for those who could afford it.

I could think of nothing worse than a dozen swans leaving poop on the floor at my wedding reception, but the man was booked out year-round, able to charge a fortune, and the swans didn't even get a cut of the money.

I steered Mindy, Amber, and Buster away from the livestock and toward Primrose's booth in the centre of the hall.

Climbing my shoulder to look over it at the swans and doves, Amber had a parting comment for them. '*I'm going to get you birdies, you bet I am.*'

'No you are not, you naughty cat,' I admonished her, picking her up to resettle her on my arms.

'*I'm a cat,*' she replied languidly. '*There is no fighting nature. I could no more resist chasing the oversized ducks than Buster could hope to form a cogent thought.*'

Poorly timed to prove Amber right, Buster said, '*Huh?*'

Ahead of me, Mindy paused. We were close to Primrose's stall now. It was gaudy and flashy, and she held centre stage on a small dais erected in the middle of her display. Tall enough to see over everyone's head, she called to any celebrities she recognised and made a big show of touting her accomplishments to draw the clients in.

The big problem with her tactic was that it worked. Her booth was twice as full as mine had been at any point and now that mine was closed, she commanded the top spot as the big wedding planner in the building.

A brief fantasy about electrocuting her to get my own back flashed through my head. I dismissed it because it was a terrible thing to think, not because I doubted I would get away with it. That's the truth and you cannot prove otherwise.

Using a tall display of cakes to hide behind, Mindy and I peered out, watching my rival reel in big fish after big fish.

'What are you gurlz doing?' squealed an excited voice from right behind us.

I almost wet myself and succeeded in losing my grip on Amber. She hit the floor and took off, shooting under the counter in the blink of an eye.

'Gurlz?' questioned Mindy, sniggering when she turned around to see who it was.

'Yeah, gurlz.' The young man to my front clicked his fingers in the air and adjusted his handbag. 'It's gurlz with a zee. It's a new term I have coined specifically to include boys like me.'

I didn't know who I was looking at, but Mindy appeared to. He was short for a man at maybe five feet seven which made him a lot shorter than Mindy. I don't want to categorize unfairly or inaccurately, but I assumed he was gay. The full face of makeup, bouffant hairdo and leather skirt beneath a pink silk blouse were all pointers but I told myself he could just be a colourful character. His sexual preferences notwithstanding, and not a subject I cared one jot about, he was trying to peer between us now to see what we might have been looking at.

'Gurlz you are acting all kinds of suspicious. Just who are you spying on?' he wanted to know.

'Auntie this is Philip,' Mindy introduced her friend.

'Hush your mouth,' he snapped, miming a slap in her direction. Turning to me, he extended his hand, but not in the way a person might if they wanted to shake it, but knuckles up and fingertips down like a lady might if a new acquaintance were going to kiss it. 'It's Philippe,' he corrected my niece. 'Philip is just so bland, whereas Philippe is exotic and filled with mystery. Just like me.'

I took his hand and shook it anyway. 'Pleased to meet you, Philippe. Are you working here?'

Phillipe went back to spying, acting surreptitiously even though he didn't know what he was supposed to be looking at.

'Philippe is a makeup artist,' Mindy told me. 'He was at the Steinecker wedding last month.'

24

'Oh.' A vague memory of meeting the young man swam its way through my brain.

Mindy asked him, 'Where is Henri? Shouldn't you be working right now?'

'Ha! I refuse to work for that pig. He's been cheating on me with his husband again.'

I tried to make that sentence work in my head and gave up.

'Sorry to push you away, Philippe. Mindy and I have some delicate business to attend to.' Plus, I really need to find my cat.

Buster sniffed Philippe's legs, leaving a snot trail on his leather skirt.

Philippe squealed and danced back a foot. 'Ewww.' In doing so, he knocked into a young lady whose glass of champagne spilled down the left jacket breast of the man whose arm she held.

'Watch it, you clumsy ...' the man shot around to growl his disgruntlement but ran out of words when he saw Philippe. 'Oh, God what are you? Some kind of fruit? God, I hate fruits.'

'Hey,' Mindy raised her voice. 'Do you know what century it is?'

I kind of wanted to intervene to cool things down, but also kind of didn't. The man was now glaring at Mindy and raising the hand that wasn't being held by the young lady with the empty champagne glass. To stop things from happening, I would have needed to physically get in the way and doing that was likely to get me clonked.

As the man raised his hand and went to jab a finger at Mindy, undoubtedly to be accompanied by some unpleasant words, my niece snatched it out of the air.

Her body moved so fluidly and with such precision that it was a kind of twisted pleasure to watch. The only way I can describe it was when I first saw ballet being performed. That seemingly effortless grace they demonstrate, which is nothing close to effortless I can assure you, was just like seeing Mindy perform martial arts.

In the blink of an eye, the man was standing on the tips of his toes while Mindy bent his fingers downward. She was only using one hand, the other was on her left hip which was cocked to the side and full of attitude.

'I think you owe this man an apology,' she suggested sweetly. When none came in the next half second, she increased the pressure.

'Aaaaah! I'm sorry, I'm sorry, okay? Aaaaah! Don't break my fingers, you little bit ...'

'Is there a problem here?' asked a new voice, cutting the man off before he could complete what he had to say. We all looked to find Reed, the head of hotel and event security, emerging from the crowd of people. All those around us had ground to a halt to view the spectacle.

'He was being impolite,' Mindy explained, doing her best to make herself look the victim.

The woman with the empty champagne glass had chosen to leave her man to deal with this himself and was six feet away pretending she was not involved.

Reed stepped in closer. 'I think perhaps you can let him go now, miss.' It was more command than statement.

The man in Mindy's grasp snorted through his nose to fight the pain in his tendons.

'Do as he says, you little ...'

Mindy cocked an eyebrow and bent his fingers back another inch before he could finish his sentence.

The resulting howl of discomfort was an octave higher than the previous one.

'Now then, sir,' Reed turned his attention to the much larger and older man. 'Your attitude does not seem to be helping matters.' Of Mindy he asked, 'Can you tell me what happened?'

Philippe jumped in. 'He called me a fruit. Twice.'

Reed took a moment to look Philippe up and down – the man's outfit was designed to create comment.

More security guards arrived, finding their way to our spot to fan out around us. So much for being surreptitious, we were the main attraction in the hall.

'I'm going to let you go now,' Mindy stated firmly. 'If you attempt to strike me, if you say anything to Philippe, if the breath from your lungs grazes against my skin, I will introduce you to a level of pain you have hitherto never even dreamed about.'

I was starting to wonder if my niece had some issues to work out.

The man's eyes were bugging from his head but when Mindy let his hand go with a shove, he winced and moaned but ultimately tucked his tail between his legs and tried to escape.

'Damn, gurl!' whooped Philippe quietly. 'You have got some mad skillz!'

I wanted a quiet word with my assistant. There were several dozen potential clients in view and none of them were going to approach our booth now. If it were open, that is.

However, I didn't get to have a quiet word, because somewhere behind me an entire can of angry swan whoopass exploded.

Amongst the hissing and honking and squawking, the shouting and swearing and flapping of enormous wings, was the sound of my cat rueing the day.

We all heard her yowl. It was followed by an angry hiss and then the panicked noises of a cat attempting to be somewhere else on the planet. Anywhere would do. Anywhere but where a bevy of angry swans were going to rip her to pieces.

Philippe placed a shocked hand on his chest. 'Gurlz what is that?' he squealed excitedly. Philippe's default setting appeared to be the excited squeal.

From floor level, Buster sniggered. '*It's that cat getting eaten! Hey, Felicity, can you have her pelt turned into a small throw rug for me? I'll be a good dog for the rest of my life if you'll do that for me.*'

I shot him a mean look.

I got a raised eyebrow in return. '*What? It will give me something to use when my back-end itches. That's got to be better than your carpet, surely?*'

Ignoring my dog, I hurried toward the bedlam now drawing the attention of the entire event hall.

Cries of alarm filled the air as swans went vertical, some of them looking like they wanted to take flight to get out of the way of other swans who were most likely trying to kill my cat.

People were running away, getting distance between themselves and the winged menace. I've heard it said that a swan's wing is powerful enough to break a man's leg. I never believed it or, at least, always

29

questioned how many men had ever arrived at hospital claiming their broken femur was the result of a swan attack. However, seeing a white wing flap into the air now, I had no desire to test the theory.

Through the feet of the humans scurrying and pushing to be farther away from the giant, mad, white birds came the terrified sound of my cat.

'Feeelllliccciiitttttyyyyyyyy!'

Hearing her allowed me to relax a little since she clearly hadn't been pecked to death. I will admit, however, to feeling grave concern over her current state and wondering if she might be missing an ear or a chunk of tail.

With Buster, Mindy, and Philippe on my tail, I tracked Amber's progress through the crowd and stopped trying to fight my way through it.

She was coming to me.

Cries of, 'What was that?' as the cat shot by someone's foot, or, 'Goodness me,' or just a straightforward shriek of alarm told me when she was about to reach me, and I crouched slightly to scoop her.

Was she injured? Was she going to need veterinary treatment?

The hem of a lady's skirt flew up a foot when Amber sprinted between her legs. It caused a fresh exclamation as the shocked woman twitched and jumped, but my focus was on Amber.

Seeing me, she ran for my arms but didn't slow down. I expected her to skid to a stop so I could pick her up. Or possibly to jump into my arms.

No, she climbed me like a tree, claws out to ensure maximum purchase on my 'bark'.

It was my turn to squeal. 'Yow!' It was in deference to my surroundings, the sea of potential clients around me, and my status as wedding planner to the stars that I kept the torrent of pain-driven expletives inside my head.

Amber ran up my left arm, across my shoulder, around behind my head and up onto my skull where she clamped down hard with twenty tiny, sickle-shaped claws.

Cringing against the pain, I froze in place.

It wasn't just me though. All around me, as if someone had pressed a giant pause button, the crowd of people attending the wedding fayre were stationary. Rushing to get away from the avian menace one second, gawping at the woman with a cat for a hat the next.

I came back to upright, cooing at Amber to be calm and take her claws out of my scalp. I turned slowly about, pivoting off my heel and toe to face my niece, but before Mindy could come to my aid the one person I truly didn't wish to see arrived.

'Nice hat!' guffawed Primrose Green.

Her shriek of laughter proved infectious, and it was followed by the electronic camera shutter noise modern phones make as she started snapping pictures.

Instantly, more joined her, some undoubtedly shooting video to upload to the internet.

I begged for help, 'Mindy?' imploring with my eyes for my niece to get the cat off my head.

If the barbs digging through my skin were bad, humiliation at the hands of Primrose was ten times worse.

31

Mindy handed Buster off to Philippe, coming to my rescue as she took over the task of cooing at the traumatised cat.

Further rescue arrived, but not in the form I was expecting.

'I think that is enough now,' commanded a man's voice as he strode through the crowd to stop in front of Primrose.

His words and tone were enough to cause a pause to the barrage of photographs being snapped, but it was who he was that stopped Primrose.

'It's just a little fun, Edward,' Primrose hit him with her best smile. 'Felicity doesn't mind. Do you, Felicity?'

A dozen retorts lined up to be the first to leave my mouth. None of them were even close to polite, and I eliminated all but one.

'You are as petty and cruel as a child in a playground, Primrose,' I sneered. 'Most children grow out of the need to make themselves feel big by putting other people down. It surprises me not one bit that you haven't.'

Mindy convinced Amber's last paw to relax, her claws leaving my flesh to the accompaniment of a worrying damp, trickling feeling.

Was I bleeding?

Primrose had a frown on her face. She wanted to protest, to argue with Edward, but he was too influential, and she dare not risk ticking him off.

With a flash, her frown changed to a smile, but Edward had already turned his attention my way.

'Edward,' she called after him, raising a hopeful hand to steer his attention back to her and very much away from me.

I had Amber back in my arms and Mindy making worrying sounds as she inspected my scalp.

'Auntie you have a few holes here.'

'You hear that?' I gave Amber a squeeze to make sure she was listening to me. 'I have holes in my head. What did you learn?'

Amber had a thoughtful scowl on her face. *'More cats. Need more cats,'* she murmured.

My need to explore what she might have planned with the addition of more cats, or where these cats might be coming from had to wait because there was a human to talk to.

'Edward, so lovely to see you,' I beamed.

Edward Smallbridge owns and runs a small jewellery boutique in London's Oxford Street. We first met many years ago when I was learning my way and he was still his father's understudy. His shop, originally opened by Edward's great grandfather, had the 'By Royal Appointment' title because his grandfather was commissioned to create jewellery for Queen Victoria. He was also the jeweller trusted with checking, cleaning, and maintaining the crown jewels.

The enormous privilege such a position carried was nothing compared to the impact it had on his sales. Just to visit his shop, one had to apply weeks or months in advance. I made recommendations to many of my top clients, pushing them towards Edward because I knew he would exceed their needs.

A visit to his boutique was an experience not to be missed and that was what we were all trying to sell. It was also why Primrose was now trying to mend any damage she might have done. The slightest snub from Edward and her ability to offer her clients a package to compete with mine would suffer.

'Felicity, darling,' she cooed. 'I do hope I haven't offended you.' I had to look up at her beaming smile. She was acting as if we were best friends.

I lost my cool. 'Your face offends me, Primrose. So too your constant need to employ negative tactics rather than attempt to win by upping your game.'

Sensing there was no point trying to win me over, she switched tactic.

'You see, Edward! I am not the aggressor here.'

I wanted to retort, but Edward twisted his head, shooting her a look I couldn't see but which stopped Primrose dead in her tracks. Her mouth hung open for a second, before she thought better of whatever she might be about to say. Her jaw snapped shut, her fake smile returned, and she began to back away.

'Just a silly misunderstanding,' she lied, grinning madly at the jeweller.

He wasn't looking at her though, his focus was on me and for perhaps the first time in my life, I noticed how intense his gaze could be. His eyes were deep blue with a hint of green toward the centre. They complemented his neatly trimmed grey hair perfectly. Edward's face was kindly, but also handsome with a strong jaw and nose like an archetypal all-American athlete. At five feet ten inches he was neither tall nor short, but he was roughly my age and looking into his eyes, I felt an unexpected tug of ... something.

34

'Can I assume this is your cat?' he asked.

Glancing down to see what he was looking at, I had completely forgotten I held Amber in my arms.

'Um, yes?' I replied as a question, which made Edward chuckle.

'You don't seem too sure,' he smiled, reaching out to stroke Amber's head.

Buster nudged Edward's leg, and sat on his rump to waft a paw in a playful way.

'*I'm Buster,*' he announced, not that anyone other than me understood what he said.

'This is Buster,' I mumbled, trying to get my jaw muscles to work right. What was happening to me?

Lifting his eyes away from Buster to meet mine again, Edward said, 'I heard about the terrible accident in your booth.'

I so desperately wanted to tell him Primrose was behind it and that it was no accident at all. I restrained my tongue instead, knowing I wouldn't need to tell anyone if I could find the proof. Her arrest would spread through our community like wildfire.

Behind me, I could hear Mindy and Philippe jabbering in animated whispers. They were like two schoolgirls watching one of their friends talk to a boy for the first time and my self-consciousness kicked in.

'I, ah … Thank you for stepping in like that Edward. It was most gracious of you. Primrose and I …' I fought for the right term, one which would not make me sound petty and inferior.

Edward held up his hand. 'Primrose is a bully, Felicity. I have observed her tactics before. I am certain you could have handled things yourself; I wouldn't want you to see me as a chauvinist rushing to the aid of a woman. I was simply there, and seeing you,' his eyes bored into mine, 'I could not stand by.'

There were more squeaks of excited encouragement from the 'gurlz' behind me. I ignored them. Edward was flirting with me, I'm not so old and so out of practice that I could confuse it with anything else. He had never married, I knew that much, and I was prepared to consider myself single, if not necessarily on the market.

A widow for several years, I told myself I could love again, but the thought of taking the step and actually declaring my interest in a man was a terrifying concept. Vince, the utter rogue that he was, acted as if our coupling were an inevitability I was foolish to resist. We even went on a date, sort of. That I was coerced into it, and we got arrested before the starters were served nullified it in my opinion. However, I didn't shout too loudly about that in case he agreed and claimed I still owed him a date.

I needed to say something. Why were my lips not working?

When I said nothing in response, Edward dipped his head in a salute.

'I must return to my stand, Felicity. Will you be reopening yours tomorrow?'

At last, a question I could answer.

'Yes, we are,' supplied Mindy, appearing by my side, and jumping in to answer before I could. 'Mrs Philips is staying here at the hotel this weekend too and has no one to take her to dinner tonight.'

My eyes flared with diabolical embarrassment and my cheeks felt hot enough to catch fire. I was going to kill Mindy when I got her somewhere private.

Edward, though, was not embarrassed. If anything, he was excited.

'Dinner?' he questioned. 'I must admit I find it shocking you do not have a line of suitors queuing for the privilege of your company, Felicity.'

I turned my head to glare at my niece, but she had already withdrawn, darting back to join Philippe where her co-conspirator felt it necessary to congratulate her. He showed me a thumbs up when I caught his eye.

Huffing a hard breath as I twisted my torso back to face Edward, I said, 'Thank you, Edward, that is most kind of you. I'm sorry to say ...'

'Someone beat me to it,' he cut over the top of me. 'Of course, Felicity, say no more.'

'No, it's not ...'

'Ah. Yes, silly Edward. You are fulfilled by your life and have no need of a man at this time.'

'Well, I wouldn't exactly say ...'

'I'm too old?' he questioned, becoming baffled now by what message I might be trying to convey.

'Goodness, no,' I stuttered.

'Too portly?' he patted his belly which was barely even there.

Mindy stepped in again. 'Wow, you two are making this look difficult. It's like trying to give Amber a pill.' Facing Edward, she said, 'Mrs Philips is staying in room 345 on the third floor. She will meet you for cocktails and dinner at eight thirty in the hotel restaurant.'

Edward and I both stared at her, utterly speechless.

'There,' Mindy rolled her eyes. 'How hard was that.' Returning to stand next to Philippe, she called over her shoulder. 'It's just dinner. Relax and have a conversation.'

Flustered, unsure what the right response was, but certain refusing to meet him now would be like slapping his face, I repeated what my niece said.

'It's just dinner.'

Edward wrestled his own features under control, his easy smile returning. 'I shall look forward to it, Felicity. Eight thirty in the restaurant?'

'Eight thirty,' I confirmed.

There followed a few seconds of uncomfortable silence while we stared at each other, each waiting for the other to say something. Naturally, we both then spoke at the same time.

'I really must be ...' he started.

His sentence got cut short when I blurted, 'I'm afraid I have ...'

We both stopped speaking, using hand gestures, and nodding to impart that we had things to do and ought to be doing them. Spinning around to walk away, I was met with the cheesy grins Mindy and Philippe sported.

'Ooh, gurl, you're gonna get some action tonight,' cheered Philippe, with an odd hand gesture that looked like he was smacking a horse on the rump. I had not the faintest idea what that was supposed to impart and did not wish to find out.

'I most certainly will not,' I declared, frankly horrified at the notion. Scowling at Mindy, I said, 'I believe you and I need to have a conversation.'

Mindy wasn't paying me any attention though. She was looking through the cake shop again and beyond to Primrose's stall.

Gesturing for me to come closer with one hand, she hissed, 'She's on the move, Auntie.'

Primrose Green was indeed on the move. My tall, elegant, and ultimately evil rival was striding across the hall with purpose. It was impossible to tell where she was heading, though the restrooms seemed a likely bet, but her destination didn't matter because I had spotted something that did.

'She's not carrying her handbag,' I pointed out.

Mindy twisted her head around to question why that was important.

I explained my reasoning, but I did it while abandoning our cover behind the cake stand to make my way to Primrose's booth.

'She had it with her when she came to our booth. She was there right before that poor Douglas Irwin got electrocuted and that means whatever tool she used to cut through the cable has got to be in it.' Like me, Primrose wore a fitted dress – there were no pockets to hide anything in, and had there been, a tool would have stuck out a mile.

'You're going to swipe her handbag?' gasped Philippe. 'Mindy your aunt is gangsta!'

'Gangsta?' I questioned, looking over my shoulder and frowning at the makeup artist.

Mindy nodded. 'Truly gangsta.'

Their abominable torturing of the English language aside, I was nothing of the sort. I was a woman with just purpose. Primrose Green had caused the death of a man and I wasn't going to let her get away with it. The awful woman acted as if her conscience were clear.

Buster, his lead still secure in Mindy's grip, tugged to get ahead of me.

*'I'll get the handbag, Felicity. This is a job for Devil Dog.'*

I was about to argue, but to snatch the bag, what I wanted was a distraction and that was one thing my pets excelled at creating.

Pausing while still ten yards from Primrose's booth, I fixed Mindy with another scowl.

I got her innocent face smiling back at me.

'I need a distraction,' I announced meaningfully. 'Get everyone in Primrose's booth to face out the front. I expect Primrose left her handbag behind the counter at the back.'

'What do you want us to do?' Mindy questioned.

I handed Amber to Philippe and shifted my gaze down to Buster. 'Are you ready to be Devil Dog?'

Buster barked his response raucously, his stumpy tail thumping a staccato beat on the floor.

Laughing wearily to myself, I said to Mindy, 'Just let him off the lead. Buster will do the rest. Just be there to round him up once I am out of Primrose's booth with her bag.'

As we broke to go in different directions, I felt a faint fluttering of nerves. I was about to do something I could not imagine entertaining under any other circumstances. Taking Primrose's bag was not stealing, I told myself, it was gathering evidence. The ends justified the means.

It's funny how much trouble such a simple thought can make.

Just as she would have wanted it, Primrose's booth occupied centre stage in the middle of the hall. It was just one of the display stands in the centre ring, all of which had a distinct front edge as they backed onto each other to form a square.

Hiding in the booth next to hers – a crazy-expensive dressmaker who I often sent my clients to visit, I pretended to examine a silk gown while I waited for mayhem to ensue.

I did not have to wait long.

Given free rein to wreak havoc, Buster bulldozed his way through a stand on the opposite side of the passage passing between the various stands. I should have seen it coming, but where I envisaged my dog perhaps knocking over a display stand of brochures or maybe just running around barking to draw attention his way, he chose instead to aim his efforts at a stall displaying cakes.

The stall holders were not known to me, which meant they had to be new to the wedding scene. It looked to be two ladies, a woman and her adult daughter perhaps. They had an elegantly decorated booth and must have paid handsomely for it given the prime position it commanded.

All that meant nothing to my block-headed Bulldog, who charged through their booth intent on destruction.

I couldn't see Buster. However, much like Amber's escape from the swans, I was able to track his progress by the squeals of surprise. Oh, yes, and then by the flying cupcakes as he slammed into the ladies' centre display with appalling consequences.

Cringing, as I acknowledged there would be a need for a humble apology and a method of making amends, I got a glimpse of Buster as he tore out the far side of the cupcake ladies' booth with no fewer than three cupcakes jammed in his mouth.

Whatever else I could accuse him of achieving, he certainly created a distraction. No one in Primrose's booth was looking my way. No one was looking at anything apart from the ornate cupcakes raining back down to earth.

I stole into her booth around the back, spotted her designer label Flirkin bag under the counter where I imagined it would be, and as nonchalantly as I could, I hooked it over my shoulder and strolled back the way I had come.

Across the way, Mindy was looking flustered and apologetic as she tried to explain Buster's behaviour.

'He slipped out of my hand,' I heard her say. She had both hands held against the sides of her crimson face and I felt good because she deserved it. Setting me up for a date without consulting me. Railroading me into it, in fact. The fact that I felt a mild tremor of excitement at meeting Edward for dinner notwithstanding, she had no right to act on my behalf and could pay the price by suffering public humiliation.

Philippe had hung back, still holding Amber in his arms as she watched the proceedings with disdain and disinterest, and so he saw me, and the bag hooked over my arm, and knew it was time to wrap things up.

Buster reappeared at my side, cake crumbs tumbling from his jowls as he scoffed down the last of the cupcakes. He had frosting on his nose and in the fur above his eyebrows.

'Has that filled your belly?' I asked flippantly.

'*Not even slightly,*' Buster replied. '*Do you think I can go back for more?*'

'No.'

'*But they won't want them now,*' he whined.

'No.'

'*Humans are fickle like that,*' he continued to argue. '*Once food has rolled around in the dirt and fluff a little and gained some texture to go with the flavour, none of you will eat it.*'

'No.'

'*Just one?*' He was looking back over his shoulder, undoubtedly calculating his chances of gobbling more cake before I could stop him. '*I'm just going to check on Mindy,*' he lied.

Mercifully, because if Buster bolted, I was never going to be able to catch him, Mindy reappeared through the press of people.

'Oh, my gosh that was sooooo embarrassing,' she gasped, her hands still clutching the sides of her face.

'Really, was it?' I enquired, my voice filled with honey. 'Would you say it was as embarrassing as having your teenage niece organising dates without being asked?'

Mindy dropped her hands and gave me a cross face. 'Oh, Auntie, all I did was help. He was soooo totally trying to ask you out.'

'Damn skippy he was,' agreed Philippe.

'You stay out of this,' I scowled at our unexpected extra. 'What are you still doing following us around anyway? Don't you have work to do?'

Philippe handed Amber back to me when I held out my arms. 'I told you, I ain't going back to no man who cheats on me.'

'With his own husband?' I wanted to be clear on the facts and this one seemed pertinent.

'Mm-hmm,' agreed Philippe, completely missing my point. 'Besides, you gurlz are crazy. I haven't had this much fun in weeks.'

We were sauntering through the hall, acting like we hadn't just stolen a bag when there were suddenly security guards running toward us.

My heart stopped for a second. How could I be busted already? When it restarted a moment later, it was beating at five times its usual speed.

Oh, my God, I was going to jail, and Primrose would get to plan the royal wedding and gloat at me for the rest of my life. An image of her linked hand in hand with the prince and his bride as they ate cake and sipped champagne on the other side of my cell bars swam though my head.

I felt sick.

But the security men were not running at me, I realised. They were rushing to get somewhere but coming closer, neither man's eyes were looking my way.

Of course, I chose that moment to catch my toe on a raised piece of the floor. I pitched forward, my centre of balance extending way beyond my front foot. I ought to have been pinwheeling with my arms but holding Amber, who I could feel tensing her muscles and getting ready to climb my head again, I was unable to do anything to stop myself from falling.

Mindy cried out something, darting forward to grab me no doubt but she would not be able to get to me in time.

However, the two men from event security saw me falling. They were about to run by, aiming to pass either side as they hurried to wherever they were needed, but both chucked out their anchors to brake themselves and catch me.

Amber swore and hissed but remained in my grip as helpful hands supported my shoulders and stood me upright once more. Primrose's Flirkin bag fell from my shoulder, catching awkwardly on my right forearm.

'Here, madam, let me help you,' offered the guard to my left, taking the weight of the Flirkin so I could juggle the cat a little and get the bag back onto my shoulder.

'Two handbags?' commented the guard to my right as he noticed I still had my own handbag looped around my body.

His eyebrow was raised in question but if he wanted to ask me something, he got cut off by his radio squawking.

'Jessop, Friday, where are you. Get to the Green booth now.' The voice was that of Reed, the head of security. He was at Primrose's booth and that had to mean she had already noticed her handbag was missing.

The guards left me now that I was back on my feet and sped off once more, weaving through the wedding fayre visitors as fast as they could.

I shot wide eyes at Mindy. 'We need to go!'

No further words were required. Primrose would hear about the dog wreaking havoc in the stall opposite hers and accuse me in a heartbeat. A few minutes ago, I was all about swiping the bag and finding some evidence to prove her guilt. Now I had to work out how to get the bag back to her booth without getting caught along the way.

I was all but running when I got to the edge of the hall and the doors to the hotel. Despite my fear of getting caught with a stolen, highly desirable, Flirkin bag, I was far more worried about letting Primrose Green get away with murder. I was going to find somewhere private and rifle through the contents of her bag.

If there was a clue in it, so help me, I was going to find it.

At the doors, we bumped into Melissa, the deputy manager of the hotel.

'Mrs Philips,' she gasped at seeing how fast we were moving.

The bag was tucked under my right arm to make it less visible but with Melissa to my front, I quickly shuffled it backward, passing it behind me to Mindy where I could use my body to hide the stolen item.

'Is everything all right?' Melissa wanted to know, concern etched into her face.

'Yes, yes,' I snapped a little too quickly. 'We, um. We missed lunch,' I clutched at the first idea that came into my head. 'Yes, we missed lunch. That terrible incident just threw us completely, but we are starving now, and we thought maybe we could have a nice meal in the wonderful restaurant you have here.'

Mindy mumbled something I couldn't make out. Her tone was urgent, so I leaned my head her way to encourage her to repeat what she said.

'Don't embellish, Auntie. You are gabbling and sound guilty.' Mindy whispered so Melissa wouldn't hear her.

I laughed, pretending that Mindy had said something funny.

47

I tried to find a way out of the conversation, my brain convinced the guards had to be looking for me already. 'Mindy was just reminding me about the accident earlier.' I explained away my laughter.

Melissa's eyes widened. 'The one where the man died? Is that funny now?'

'No,' I replied instantly resetting my face to sombre and sorrowful.

Mindy mumbled quietly, 'Somebody shoot me, please.'

'*I need to go outside*,' demanded Buster, tugging Mindy's arm as he tried to get ahead of me.

Finally finding a reason to excuse myself, I relayed Buster's demand, 'I need to take my dog outside. Can we catch up later?'

Mindy grabbed my right bicep, gripping it tightly and using it to steer me around the confused event organiser.

I waved a hurried goodbye and let Mindy and Philippe escort me from the wedding fayre and into the hotel lobby.

'Restroom,' Mindy pointed, shoving me in the direction of the ladies'.

'*I really do need to go outside*,' said Buster, adding a plaintive whine to his request. '*Those cupcakes were more filling than I realised.*'

I swore inside my head, flipping mental coins and calculating outcomes.

'Sorry, Buster, you'll have to hold it.'

'*Hold it?*' he questioned, sounding worried.

We scooted across the lobby, doing our best not to attract attention though I was convinced everyone was looking at me and could see the guilt hanging over me like a shroud.

Mindy got to the restroom door first, barging into it and tugging Buster after her. Philippe was right on her heel until I stopped him.

'This is the ladies',' I pointed out.

He flicked his head to send his bouffant hair away from his face. 'Where do you think I usually go, girlfriend? Us gurlz always go together.'

Now I was stuck. Philippe, despite all the makeup, hair, and ladies' clothing, looked and sounded like a man. What was the right thing to do here? Truth be told, I needed to use the restroom myself, and wasn't comfortable doing so with a man outside my stall door.

'Um, do you still have …' I flicked a finger in the direction of where his wotsits ought to be while questioning what the right term to use might be.

'My junk?' he employed a word I would not be comfortable using, but was helpful, nevertheless. 'Yes, sugar. I'm gay, not transgender, but I do come with a side order of crossdressing. Philippe has a style that is all his own. Now get your sexy butt in here so we can see what's in that bag.'

He pushed through the door without another word, leaving me with little choice but to follow.

Huffing at how my day was going, I followed my assistant and the latest member of my entourage into the restroom.

Thankfully, it was devoid of life. I put Amber down, letting the lazy cat stretch her legs for however long this took since she could not now escape.

49

Mindy had found a supply of cleaning things which included a sign advising the toilets were out of use.

She pried the door open, peeked to make sure no one was looking and put the sign outside the restroom.

Then, for good measure, Phillippe used a mop handle against a stall door to jam the door shut.

I allowed myself a small sigh of relief.

Mindy still had the Flirkin, but it was on the fold-out baby change table now where she unceremoniously upended it, spilling its contents.

All three of us gathered around, examining the detritus now covering the baby change table. It was nothing out of the ordinary. Keys, a purse with credit cards and a few twenty pound notes. A pack of tissues, an unopened box of tampons.

Mindy picked up Primrose's phone. 'You could delete all her contacts, Auntie.'

It was tempting. However, I got to where I am by being good at what I do. Dirty tactics and negative press are Primrose's tools. I would never stoop to her level just as I doubt she can never elevate herself to mine.

I rooted through the rest of it, opening the trashy erotic novel she was part way through – she'd turned down the corner of a page like a heathen Neanderthal – just to make sure there wasn't a hole cut in the pages to hide a set of wire strippers.

A lipstick, a bottle of perfume, the list of items went on but the only thing I could find that could conceivably be used to bare the wire inside the cable was a nail file.

And I just couldn't convince myself I was looking at what was effectively a murder weapon.

It was a bust. The guards were probably looking for me and I had exposed myself to countless problems if I got caught with Primrose's bag for nothing.

Not nothing, I told myself. I had eliminated one place where she might have hidden the tool she used, but that didn't mean we were beaten.

Picking up the one item from Primrose's bag that might prove useful, I held it aloft. With sparkling eyes, I said, 'The game is still afoot.'

Both the young people gave me a bewildered look.

'A foot?' asked Mindy. 'You mean as in twelve inches because I'm a millennial, Auntie. Feet and inches and all that old money stuff doesn't mean a whole lot to me.'

'Nor me,' agreed Philippe. 'Or did you mean that we have to get on our feet?' he speculated.

I knew young people were prone to live their lives on their phones and I carried the impression they read far less than I used to at their age, but had they honestly never seen a Sherlock Holmes movie?

Dropping my Basil Rathbone act – it's not as if either Mindy or Philippe would have any idea who that was – I gave it to them in simpler terms. We have her door key. If there is no evidence here, maybe we can find it in her room.'

'Aren't you worried the guards are looking for you because they saw you with the bag?' asked Philippe.

'Yes,' I agreed. 'But I doubt they will be looking in her room.'

Mindy poked her head out of the restroom door, and immediately yanked it back in again.

Leaning her back against the door, she said, 'There's gotta be half a dozen of those rentacop security guards out there,' she reported.

I felt a ball of worry form in my gut. How were we going to get out of this? Primrose was bound to have pointed the finger at me and for once she was right to do so. If hotel security caught me with the bag, I was a thief. If we abandoned the bag or dropped it out of a window, they would find it eventually and my fingerprints and DNA were all over it. No amount of hand gel and sanitising wipes were going to change that.

'*I really need to go,*' whined Buster. '*Seriously now. I can't hold it much longer.*'

Problems were just mounting one on top the other.

'*It would be easier to just kill the dog, don't you think?*' suggested Amber. 'It would solve his problem and *I'll be happier, that's for sure.*'

I didn't expect it, but it was Philippe who came to my rescue with an idea that would never have occurred to me.

'You could just buy another bag,' he remarked. 'They have them for sale in the hotel lobby boutique.'

Mindy and I both stared at him.

'This bag?' I pointed to the one-of-a-kind Flirkin.

'Yes,' he nodded.

'This exact bag?'

'Yes.'

'They are one of a kind,' I argued.

'Na-uh,' Philippe shook his head vigorously. 'That's what Flirkin want you to think. Mostly their bags are one of a kind, but sometimes they do a limited edition run of a single design. It's way cheaper and they sell like hotcakes.'

'And they have them here?' Mindy questioned.

'They did this morning,' Philippe defended his claim. 'I don't know if they still do, because … like I said … they sell like hotcakes.'

This could really work. The guards had seen me with a bag that they were now looking for. If I turned up with one that I had a receipt for, I was home free. This was totally going to work. I yanked my purse from my handbag, selected a credit card and handed it to Philippe.

'Quick as you can, Philippe, get me a replacement bag.'

'What if they have sold out?'

'Get me one that looks as close to this as you can,' I begged, saying a silent prayer that I might catch a little bit of luck.

With Mindy checking the coast was clear, Philippe snuck out.

Buster tried to jam his head through the gap and got it wedged when Mindy closed the door as swiftly as she could.

Thus ensued a farcical episode as Mindy tried to shut the door before the guards noticed, Buster continued trying to get out so he could find some lawn on which to relieve himself, and I had to grab the daft dog's legs and haul him back across the tile.

'*But I can't hold it,*' Buster wailed.

'What's the matter with him?' asked Mindy.

'He needs to go potty,' I explained.

'*I really, really do,*' Buster whined.

Mindy skewed her lips to one side, sizing up the problem and looking for a workable solution. 'Hold him over the toilet?'

She looked about as uncertain as I felt. The likely outcome of such a venture had poop-ridden disaster written all over it.

Looking about the restroom for some means of salvation, a lightning bolt of inspiration hit me.

Crouching down to get in Buster's face as he panted and tensed his muscles, I said, 'Remember when you were a puppy?'

'*I guess,*' he panted, his face a mask of worried concentration.

'I used to put puppy pads down in the kitchen for you, yes?'

'*That's right,*' Buster wheezed and winced.

Bouncing back onto my feet, I started tearing sheets from the hand towel dispenser. Laying them on the tile, I soon had an appropriately sized target zone for Buster's back end. Putting him at one end of the room, Mindy and I retreated as far as we could then huddled by the door and got ready to hold our noses.

'*This is so disgusting,*' commented Amber, flicking her tail, and refusing to watch.

Unable to hold it back any longer, Buster hunched over. Ten seconds later, he trotted away looking happy and relieved and Mindy and I questioned how long we could hold our breath.

Not long enough was the answer.

Without taking a breath, Mindy squeaked, 'It feels like my eyeballs are melting.'

A shunt against the door we were leaning on startled us both.

Despite the sign outside, someone was trying to get in.

My pulse jumped again.

'Gurlz, let me in,' hissed Philippe.

The moment I got out of the way, Mindy pulled the door open just enough to let Philippe in.

'I got it!' he exclaimed excitedly, holding up an elegant cardboard bag with little rope handles and the name 'Flirkin' on the side. Unfortunately for Philippe he hadn't noticed that we were holding our breaths.

I could feel my pulse beginning to bang inside my skull as I starved my brain of oxygen, but as Philippe turned green and started to choke, I decided to hold on a little longer.

'Oh, my God! What is that smell?'

'Aunt Felicity farted,' laughed Mindy, amusing herself immensely but in so doing also taking a breath and then regretting it.

I pointed a hand at the puppy pad and the obvious towering brown mountain sitting atop it, then opened the door a crack and sucked in as much clean air as I could.

Seeing my tactic, Mindy joined me, jamming her head into the gap just above mine. Philippe got on his hands and knees to get in under me which is how all three of us saw that we were busted.

Whether it was Philippe and Mindy choking to death or the door opening and closing that drew the guards' attention to us, we had been spotted and there were curious people coming our way.

We had twenty seconds to come up with a plan.

Hurriedly, and holding our breath again though the diabolical funk was beginning to clear, we shoved all of Primrose's belongings back into her bag.

When Philippe shrieked unexpectedly and started laughing, I almost wet myself and slapped him hard on the arm.

'What the heck, Philippe?'

'It's a fake!' he continued to laugh. 'Her bag is a knock off. This couldn't have cost more than twenty-five bucks.'

'How can you tell?' Mindy wanted to know, dropping the last of Primrose's things into it.

Philippe took my brand new Flirkin bag out of its wrapper, gently stroking the fine leather as if it were a pet to be loved.

'This one has the pattern on the lining.' He opened my bag to show us, then pointed to Primrose's. 'This one does not.'

Primrose's bag did indeed not have a patterned lining, nor did the leather feel as supple. It really summed her up: fake.

A polite knock on the door got us moving again.

'Ladies?' a hesitant voice called around the side of the door as it opened a crack.

'Do you mind?' snapped Mindy.

Philippe nodded his head toward Buster's offering. 'What do we do about that?'

Okay, so it was much larger than the mess I had to deal with when he was a puppy, but the principle was the same. I was going to flush it.

Holding my breath, I folded the layers of paper hand towel inward, but as I encased the towering mountain of poop and trapped the stench inside, I worried that the thicker towels might block the plumbing. I didn't want to be responsible for flooding the hotel lobby. I was having enough of a day of it already.

Besides, a far more evil plan had just hatched inside my head.

The door opened a little farther.

'Ladies, I need to ask you to vacate this restroom, please.'

I recognised the voice now. It was Reed. And I recognised the next voice when it spoke too.

'Oh, for goodness sake, man. Get out of my way!' raged Primrose. 'I'm telling you that awful woman has been trying to steal my business for years. Now that she is losing because I am simply better than her, she has resorted to stealing my things.'

Primrose was about to come in, but I was going to beat her to it.

The clicking of her heels on the marble outside allowed me to time my exit to arrive right in her face. The effect would have been more pleasing if I didn't have to strain my neck to look up into her annoying face, but I took what I had and worked with it.

'Is there something you want, Primrose?'

59

Her eyes went about as wide as they could when she spotted the bag on my shoulder. She lunged for it with both hands.

'I want my bag back, you thief!' she shrieked.

I ducked under her arms, squealing in fright. Okay, so I was feigning it, but I made it sound convincing.

In my arms, Amber hissed on cue, adding drama.

'Grab her!' commanded Primrose, spinning on her heels as she tried to catch me.

The guards were gathered in one spot which gave me lots of escape routes. However, I didn't plan to go very far.

As the guards fanned out to cut me off, I decided I was far enough away from the restroom door and stopped.

Everyone was wheeling around to face me, which meant they were no longer paying attention to the toilet.

'Where's her niece?' snapped Primrose, twisting to look back at the restroom door.

Now surrounded by a loose circle of security guards and the two cops, I made sure to look worried – I needed Primrose to believe she had the upper hand.

Primrose grabbed the sleeve of a hotel security guard, dragging him with her as she went back to check the restroom … which opened before she could get to it.

Buster's snuffling snout exited first, his taut lead ending when Mindy's hand arrived. My tall, athletic niece stepped out and looked at Primrose with a warning glare.

'What is happening?' she demanded to know.

Primrose, her ire up and far too used to snapping at people and having them comply, reached out to grab Mindy's wrist. She intended to drag her over to where I was so she could have the guards interrogate us both.

'Your aunt is a common thief!' Primrose declared. 'And you are undoubtedly her accomplice.' Her eyes were already swinging back to accuse me, her hand expecting to find Mindy's arm and grasp it.

Mindy only moved the one arm, whipping it up and then down again to block Primrose. In so doing, she whacked Primrose on the meaty part of her forearm and my nemesis shrieked in pain.

'She hit me!' Primrose exclaimed loudly. 'Do something! The dirty little criminal hit me!'

Reed had watched the debacle for long enough.

'Okay, I think we should all take it down a gear.' He manoeuvred himself to get between Primrose and Mindy who was trying hard not to grin. With his arms raised, he cocked an eyebrow at Primrose. 'Please. We can get to the bottom of this without need for further drama.'

'*Want me to pee up her leg?*' asked Buster.

I flared my eyes at Buster, unable to directly respond to his question with so many people around and refocused my attention on Primrose as she stalked toward me rubbing her forearm. Her face was set to an unpleasant smirk – she was looking forward to the next few minutes.

Attempting to reassert her dominance, Primrose stopped rubbing her arm and held it up, beckoning, 'Hand it over then.'

'My bag?' I questioned.

Primrose turned scarlet. 'My bag!'

I tilted my head, aiming for a blend of curious and befuddled with my body language and facial expression. Mindy walked around the back of Primrose, coming to stand by my side.

'You want my handbag?' I questioned.

Primrose almost exploded.

'IT'S MY HANDBAG!' she screamed, spittle flying from her lips as her head did a commendable impression of a beetroot. Her right foot started to move, her intention to rip the handbag from my body quite clear to anyone looking.

The volume of her shriek had already ensured everyone was looking and we were in the hotel lobby still. Off to one side, but visible to everyone passing through, I thought I spotted Kanye West looking our way. This was not the sort of behaviour the Randecaux Hotel would tolerate.

Reed stepped forward, raising an arm to halt Primrose before she could get moving.

'Now then, Mrs Green,' he warned respectfully. Switching his focus to look at me, his expression was apologetic. 'I'm sorry, Mrs Philips, may I please inspect your handbag.'

'My handbag,' insisted Primrose again, her rage barely held in check.

'You have a new Flirkin like mine?' I questioned my rival, surprise showing on my brow.

'That one *is* mine,' growled Primrose.

Goodness, I was enjoying this. Did it make me a bad person? Probably, yes. Did I care? Not one bit.

Primrose chose to go with an insult. 'You don't have the style to be able to carry off such a bag.'

I cocked my hip to one side. 'And you don't have the money to buy one. Is yours the genuine article?' I was watching Primrose's eyes, so I saw when the flicker of fear pass through them.

'Of course, it's the real thing,' she lied. 'What do you take me for?'

Mindy answered for me. 'A scummy cow with a flabby bum held in by supportive pants?'

The scarlet returned to Primrose's face as the volcano inside her blew its stack. She surged forward and had to be held back by Reed and another security guard.

When she settled again, I noted she was clenching her cheeks and trying to stand a little taller.

'Mrs Philips,' Reed addressed me again. 'I really must insist.'

I nodded, slipping the bag off my shoulder. Philippe had waited a minute as we suggested he should, then slipped out of the ladies' restroom. It happened a few seconds ago when Primrose was trying to get to me again and no one noticed him. I saw him leave the hotel lobby via the doors to get back to the wedding fayre and knew it was time to play the masterstroke.

Meeting Primrose's angry glare with a sad expression, I held the bag at my side not quite ready to hand it over.

'I'm afraid, I haven't been entirely truthful, Reed,' I admitted.

'Ha! Now she admits it,' laughed my rival, smiling now that she could taste victory coming.

'I spotted Mrs Green's handbag and know enough about such things that I could tell it was a fake straight away.'

Primrose's smile froze.

'It's not a fake,' she lied again.

'Does it have the patterned liner?' I asked and held her gaze, waiting for a reply. When she failed to respond, Reed and everyone else turned their attention her way.

I repeated my question, framing it differently. 'What is the pattern on the liner of the genuine article, Primrose? Do you know?'

I reached inside the bag, withdrawing my hand slowly with my receipt trapped between two fingers. I hadn't looked at it until this point, and seeing the number displayed at the bottom, I choked.

Philippe had said the Flirkin bags on sale here were a limited edition run and were cheaper than a standard Flirkin because they were not made to order. I had no idea what a normal Flirkin cost, but I could swap this for a car.

Getting my face back under control, I addressed the head of hotel security and managed to sound just a touch ashamed when I admitted, 'The boutique in the hotel lobby is selling a limited edition Flirkin bag. You can call me petty, but when I spotted Mrs Green, a long-time rival, with her fake bag, I chose to buy myself the real thing.'

I held up the receipt for Reed to see, trusting that he would not scrutinise it carefully enough to spot the time stamp on it was ten minutes old.

Primrose visibly trembled in her effort to control her rage.

'She's lying,' Primrose accused.

'You never did answer my question about the liner, Primrose. Can you describe the pattern? I don't think you can because yours doesn't have one. It is a sure-fire giveaway that the bag is a fake. Whereas mine ...' I turned over the top edge so everyone could see the Flirkin logo embroidered all over the lining, '... is the real McCoy.'

'So hop it, you sour faced old trout,' added Mindy with a sneering smile.

Primrose looked about ready to kill. She didn't believe I was innocent. Not for one minute, but what could she do?

Apparently, she could lunge for the receipt in Reed's hand.

'Let me see that!' she yelled, barging through the one guard still blocking her path. He'd not been paying enough attention and wound up falling on his backside as she dove for the receipt.

Reed whipped it away like big kid teasing a younger sibling by holding a ball out of their reach. Since it was near to me, I plucked it from his fingers and put it back in my bag.

'That is enough now, Mrs Green,' Reed warned. 'I believe you owe Mrs Philips an apology.'

'Ha! Just because she has you fooled, you ... you idiot,' Primrose was beyond reason and willing to lash out at anyone.

I chose to press my advantage. 'Primrose you don't like me, do you?'

'I loathe you. You are everything this industry doesn't need.'

I took her comment to mean that the industry didn't need someone better than her because it affected her top line.

'You would happily see me fail, yes?'

'I would give anything to see you no longer able to steal my clients.'

I really wanted to argue that my clients are not stolen. They are not romanced, coerced, or bribed either, but that wasn't the point of my question.

Making sure everyone was listening, I asked, 'Primrose, what were you doing hanging around my booth right before the accident earlier?'

Of the people around us, about half looked at me in surprise. The other half looked at Primrose and they were wondering what her next words might be.

I think she had something unpleasant poised on her lips, but her brain worked out what I was suggesting, and then she saw the security team looking at her. Their expressions had changed.

'You can't … I had nothing to do with what happened,' she stammered.

'What did you use to cut the cable, Primrose?'

'Oh, no you don't, you little troublemaker.' She emphasised the *little* as much as she could. 'I only came to your puny little booth so that I could make fun of it. I would have no idea how to cut a cable and electrocute someone.'

She wasn't able to present a convincing argument and even more of the people around her were now looking her way. Their eyes were silently judging her – was she a person capable of murder?

'What happened to your handbag, Primrose? Was there evidence in it?' I was on a roll now, accusing her because I knew she was guilty. I had not one bit of proof, but as she took a step back and found two members of the security team behind her, she looked guilty. 'Did you throw it away and then try to cover that up by telling people I stole it?' My voice was getting louder.

'Don't be …'

'… ridiculous?' I cut her off, my voice louder than hers. 'You just said you would do anything to see me fail. You came to my booth to sabotage it,' I reminded everyone. 'I am your biggest rival, isn't that right, Primrose? I steal your clients, isn't that the claim you made?' I was advancing toward her, my hand up and accusing. 'Maybe murder wasn't your intention.' In truth, I suspected her aim was to cut the supply to my chiller so I would be serving warm champagne instead of cold. Intention hardly mattered when a man had died. 'Whatever it was you wished to achieve, Primrose, the end result is the same.' I quietened my voice and adopted a sombre tone. 'A man died, Primrose. You should do the decent thing and admit your part in his death.'

'But I had nothing to do with it,' she protested. All the rage and bluster was gone. Her forthright demands for justice had been turned around and the force she gathered to track me down were now aimed inwards to her.

In a quiet voice, because we were still attracting a lot of attention, Reed said, 'I think perhaps you should come with me, Mrs Green.'

He reached out a hand, inviting her to come with him.

She snatched her arm away instantly, but she was surrounded and there was nowhere for her to go.

Philippe reappeared in the doorway leading back from the wedding fayre to the lobby. I got a surreptitious thumbs up from him before he feigned interest in a display of sunglasses and effectively vanished from sight.

Primrose closed her mouth, gathering herself, and though it pains me to admit, I was impressed by her coolness when she drew herself up to full height.

'Very well,' she said, her vicious eyes attempting to burrow through me. 'It would appear you are winning this round, Felicity. But you know what they say about winning the war?'

'That it sucks to be you?' guessed Mindy.

'No,' I corrected my niece. 'That's not what they say at all.' Primrose was down, but she was going to get back up and that worried me more than I expected. As she turned to walk away in the direction Reed indicated, I could hear her calmly assuring the head of security that he had no evidence to link her to the accident because there was none.

For the first time since poor Douglas got electrocuted, I began to doubt if I was right about Primrose's guilt.

Mindy made a show of waving Primrose off. 'Bye, Felicia.'

'Who's Felicia?' I questioned with a frown.

Mindy snorted a laugh – apparently my question was amusing.

'It's just something we say, Auntie. Sometimes I forget you are the same age as my parents.'

I wanted to hit the annoyingly hip and cool teenager with a smart retort. Unfortunately, I couldn't think of one. More importantly, I had something more pressing than a witty reply.

I held aloft the one item that had not gone back into Primrose's bag – her door card - the silent action a declaration of intent to be noticed and understood by my niece – we were going to search Primrose's room.

Once Primrose, Reed, and his team departed, I waved the receipt in front of Philippe's face.

'You said these were going cheap.'

'I know,' he squealed. 'I couldn't believe the price either. That's not cheap, it's cheaper than cheap! Gurl if I had the money, I would be over there buying myself one right now.'

Philippe and I had vastly different opinions on what a functional item ought to cost. The bag was out of the box now and looped over my arm. I badly wanted to return it but would feel too ashamed.

I was stuck with it. And it wasn't even my style.

It was no surprise to me when Philippe came with us. I wasn't sure having another team member was necessary, or whether an extra pair of hands was going to help or hinder us. However, he had proven himself useful so far, and was volunteering his help so I didn't feel that I could turn him away.

I didn't know what room Primrose was staying in, but it took only a very brief conversation with one of the ladies on reception to obtain that. All I had to do was lie about she and I being friends and wanting to take her mobile phone up to her because she came over ill but left it behind when she went for a lie down.

I was getting good at subterfuge.

Inside the elevator as it travelled up, Mindy asked Philippe where he put Primrose's handbag.

'Gurl I tucked it under the counter where Felicity said she found it, but stuffed it right to the back so it would look like Primrose just didn't look hard enough for it.' Looking at me in the mirrored wall of the car, he asked, 'What's the beef between you two anyway? Did she steal your man?'

'Nothing so dramatic,' I assured him. 'I would happily pay Primrose no attention at all, but she sees my success as a challenge to her own and wants to do better by making sure I do worse.'

Philippe called her a name that would cause his hair to spontaneously ignite if repeated in church.

Mindy agreed with him. 'That is exactly what she is. A massive one.'

I wasn't going to argue but chose to remain silent.

The elevator car pinged and slowed, reaching the fifth floor where we would find Primrose's room.

Nerves crept in again as I neared her door. If she was downstairs confessing her guilt, I doubted anyone would argue that searching her room for clues was not justified. However, I not only doubted she was admitting anything, if she was guilty, I might be accused of tampering with evidence. Worse yet, if she wasn't guilty, and the niggling doubt I felt was getting stronger, then I was about to illegally enter her room.

Just like stealing her bag, and then her door card, I was committing crimes in the pursuit of justice, but I am not a detective or a private investigator. If caught, I would not be able to argue I had just cause.

As fear for what I was about to do filled my belly, I gritted my teeth and swiped the door card over the entry pad. If it clicked and turned green, I was going in.

Click. Green light.

Bother.

The young people were clearly waiting for me to grab the door handle and go in, and Buster was nudging the door with his nose, leaving wet prints behind. I huffed out a breath, pulled my hand up into my sleeve so I wouldn't leave fingerprints and pushed my way into Primrose's room.

*How many crimes can you commit in one day, Felicity?*

'What are we looking for, Auntie?'

Mindy's question was an appropriate one to pose, but I was darned if I had an answer, so I went with, 'Anything incriminating.'

Mindy and Philippe exchanged a look before they both shrugged and began to poke around. Like me, Primrose had been here a couple of days already, so her suitcase was empty, and she had a dozen outfits hanging in the room's wardrobe. Her makeup and hair care products were arranged on the dresser and there were toiletries in the sink.

I put Amber down. 'Don't go getting comfortable,' I commanded, not that I thought my cat would listen to me. Buster was snuffling off the lead. I didn't think he would lift his leg, but before I warned him not to, I decided I didn't much care if he did.

Using a tissue from my insanely expensive handbag, I made sure to avoid leaving fingerprints and DNA when I opened drawers and employed a pen to move her knickers and things around rather than touch them.

If I was hoping to find a notebook listing the methods by which she planned to thwart me and one circled that said 'electrocute a man in her booth' then I was to be severely disappointed.

I continued to poke and prod for ten minutes, but there just wasn't enough places to look. By the time I admitted defeat, Mindy, Philippe, and I had been through the same drawers, bags, and spaces more times than the task required.

Mindy was waiting for me to give up. 'It doesn't look like there is anything here, Auntie.'

I was about to start toward the door when I heard voices in the corridor outside. They were coming our way, and they were arguing.

'Are you stupid, man?' Primrose snarled. 'I already told you twice that my handbag was not there when I looked before. Felicity Philips must have put it back there while you and your idiots were interviewing me.'

I froze, my blood running cold. She had me this time for certain. How the heck was I going to explain my presence in her room. Buster's ears came up. He knew the voice too and was going to start barking.

Mercifully, Mindy knew him well enough and had the reactions to grab him before he could make a sound. With a hand clamped around his mouth, she soothed him and kept him quiet.

From her position on the floor, she asked, 'Do we hide? Or fight?'

'Fight?' I whispered incredulously. I doubted adding assault to my list of crimes would help. Hiding was the only thing I could come up with, but surely we would just get caught anyway and then look twice as guilty.

Outside in the corridor, Primrose continued to voice her opinion. 'There is nothing for you to find in my room, I can assure you.'

'Nevertheless, Mrs Green,' I heard Reed say, 'I am required to be thorough. At this time, I am still not convinced there is no reason to call the police.'

'That's because you are an idiot,' Primrose repeated herself in a bored tone. 'Oh, for goodness sake, where is my room key?'

We could all hear her groping around in her bag, trying to find the key card I held in my right hand. She couldn't get in, I breathed a sigh of relief, and they would have to get a new key from reception. The moment they moved away we would sneak out.

'And what is this?' she questioned. 'Why have I got a ball of tissues in my bag?'

I closed my eyes and cursed myself. Putting poop in her bag seemed like such a good idea at the time. Not so much now, though.

'Is it cake?' Primrose asked no one in particular.

I could picture her now. The folded-up package of tissues was probably held in the flat of one hand while she unwrapped it with the other. Mindy and Philippe had also realised what was happening and were trying to suppress their excited giggles.

'I have a master key, if you cannot find yours, Mrs Green,' advised Reed.

My heart beat out a quick staccato. Of course he had a key. They were coming in anyway and the flicker of hope I'd held died in my chest.

Sounding pleased for once, Primrose made Reed wait. 'I think one of the cake suppliers is trying to win me over. They must have dropped this off with my staff and they put it in my bag. It looks like chocolate cake,' she beamed. 'I can see where the frosting has stained the tissue.'

'Might that be why you could not find your bag, Mrs Green?' asked Reed. 'One of your staff had it and not Mrs Philips?'

'Nonsense, man!' Primrose was not going to have her opinion swayed. 'Now is it chocolate or coffee? I do hope it's not coffee.'

I held my breath until I heard the scream. Fast feet could be heard outside, all of them backing away from Primrose as she began to gag.

'It was her!' Primrose correctly identified the culprit. 'Now do you believe me? She stole my bag and now I have the evidence to prove it!'

'Poop?' questioned Reed. 'How do you propose to use that as evidence?'

'It can be DNA tested or something,' growled Primrose, sounding apoplectic now. Then I heard her gasp. 'What are you doing?'

'Getting rid of it, Mrs Green. No one is going to analyse poop and try to tie it to a supposed bag theft. Most especially since the bag is not actually missing.' I could hear Reed beginning to lose his cool. 'I am not interested in what Mrs Philips might have done. Now, Mrs Green, do you have your key, or shall I use mine? I will tolerate no further stalling.'

Primrose gasped again. 'She took it! That awful Felicity Philips stole my bag because she wanted my key! She put poop in my bag, and she could be doing goodness knows what in my room. She gasped yet again. 'I bet she's in there now! Well, don't just stand there, you idiot! Open the door!'

I had gotten so close to getting away with it. Reed believed Primrose had a case to answer. Maybe she was guilty of tampering with the refrigerator cable and maybe she wasn't, but all focus was about to swing toward me because all the things she had been saying about me were true. Getting caught in her room would cause an instant shift of opinion.

How I was going to rue the day. They were coming through that door any second now, so I prepared my face to look directly into Primrose's eyes with haughty superiority, and tried not to wet myself.

I heard the noise of a door opening behind me, but it really didn't register in my head.

'Perhaps you would like to follow me?' asked Vince, stepping into the room via a door in the wall behind me.

'*Vince!*' barked Buster.

'Did you hear that?' asked Primrose. 'That was her dog!'

Amber twitched her tail. '*Stupid dog.*'

With Buster charging to get to Vince, Mindy snatched Philippe's arm before the dog lead could go taut, and sprinted across the room, tugging the makeup artist along like a kite. I was left in the middle of the room, right in front of the door, staring dumbfounded at the private investigator.

'How?' I mumbled, too confused to form a sentence.

'No time,' replied Vince, marching across the room just as I heard the main entry door click open.

Vince scooped me into his arms and started running. I didn't want to be carried like a baby. Nor did I want the horrible rogue to touch me, but now was not the time to slap him away and loudly demand to be put down.

Now was the time to accept being rescued.

Mindy's wide eyes watched as Vince carried me through the door into the adjoining room. The moment we were through, she tried to close the door.

'Amber,' I squealed in a panicked whisper – the cat was still sitting on Primrose's bed.

The door to Primrose's room was already beginning to open. We had two seconds, if that.

Philippe bolted, hooked a hand under Amber's belly, and threw himself back through the door to the adjoining room as I heard Reed begin to speak.

'See, Mrs Green?' said Reed. 'No one here. Fan out, chaps. Search everything.'

Carefully, and as quietly as he could, Vince pushed the door between the rooms the final half inch to get it closed and we all held our breath while he turned the lock. When it gave a click only we could hear, I finally gasped some air into my lungs.

On the other side of the wall, Primrose continued to offer Reed's security team verbal abuse as they went about their business.

'That was close,' sighed Mindy in a quiet whisper. Her back was against the wall, her form slumped and sagging as the tension of such a close call seeped away. Buster's lead was in her hand, but she let it go now that we were safe.

Buster darted across the room to greet Vince, wagging his bottom so madly he was having trouble getting his back legs to work.

Vince dropped me lightly back onto my feet and backed away. Instantly, I spun around to face him, my eyes narrowed and my expression accusatory.

'What are you doing here?' I snapped.

Vince raised both his eyebrows and then both his hands as he took a pace away in mock surrender.

'I was coming to your rescue, darling.' He was smiling at me in that earnest way he always does when he is probably trying to picture me naked.

I dropped Amber gently onto the bed and growled, 'Don't call me that.'

'Sweetie?' he tried.

My eyes narrowed a little farther.

'Snookums?' Now he was trying to fight the smirk threatening to break out on his face. 'Honeybear?'

I showed him my teeth.

It only made him laugh. 'Okay, okay, Felicity,' he relented. 'I heard you were in trouble and came to offer my assistance. I believe there was an incident in your booth earlier and someone was killed.'

I held up a finger, making him stop. 'What do you mean you heard I was in trouble?'

My eyes might have been narrowed to such an extent that I could barely see, but I noticed the slight movement of Vince's eyes when he twitched them in Mindy's direction.

I spun around to glare at her. 'You told me you were sending a tweet. I knew you were acting suspicious. How could you?'

'He's a private investigator, Auntie,' she defended herself not bothering to deny her guilt. 'He knows about all this stuff.'

'Hi, I'm Philippe,' said Philippe, giving Vince a jaunty wave. With so much going on and my pulse threatening to make my heart explode, I had forgotten to introduce our newest team member.

Vince gripped the makeup artist's hand, squeezing it firmly. 'Pleased to meet you. I'm Felicity's other half.'

'No, you are not!' I blurted, failing to keep my voice down and wondering if it would draw attention from next door when I kicked Vince in his shorts.

Vince just chuckled. 'She's playing a little hard to get. It's quite sexy actually,' he confided with Philippe.

Mentally, I was using a nutcracker on something he would not want me to use it on.

Philippe bit his lip, glancing at me and then back to Vince before he said, 'You might need to up your game. Your other half has a date tonight.'

'I am not his other half!' A muscle next to my right eye twitched.

Vince frowned for a second, before his face brightened again. 'Trying to make me jealous, eh? You saucy little minx.'

Mindy rolled her eyes and started for the door, collecting Amber as she went. 'I can't listen to this. Old people flirting is soooo weird. Come on, Philippe, we need to be somewhere else. I'll drop Amber back in your room, Auntie.' She whistled for Buster. 'That way you two can … whatever.'

Obediently, Philippe followed, the two of them about to leave.

'You're not leaving me here with him,' I gasped running to get to the door first.

'Yes,' agreed Vince, 'I should probably vacate this room too, just in case the person staying here comes back.'

Mindy, Philippe, and I all stopped at the door to look at him.

'This isn't your room?' Mindy tried to clarify.

Vince frowned at her. 'Why would it be my room?'

'If it's not your room, how did you get in here?' asked Philippe.

Vince shrugged, walking toward us and the door so we could all leave. 'I'm supposed to be able to get into locked places. It goes with the job.'

I nodded my head sadly for I was already aware of his skills in such matters. A new question occurred to me, and I put my hand up to halt his progress.

'How did you know to break into this room? How could you have possibly known we were trapped next door and that there was a door between them?'

Vince chuckled again. 'I've been here half an hour, darling. When I arrived, you were in the hotel lobby surrounded by security guards and having an argument with that Primrose Green woman you hate.'

I remembered Vince met her briefly outside Maidstone police station a few weeks ago.

'You were following me,' I concluded.

'And a good thing too, wouldn't you say?' He went around me to get to the door. 'As for the adjoining rooms, that was just a guess, but when I saw the hotel security arrive, I chose to act. Some of us are just heroic that way.'

Buster joined in. *'Yeah, some of us were born to stalk the night righting wrongs and bringing justice to the shadows.'*

I rolled my eyes and wondered what I had done wrong in the past to deserve such torture now.

Vince led the way out, confident that if there were security chaps in the corridor outside, they would not give him a second look. There was no one there though, so I followed Mindy and Philippe out, carrying Amber again, and letting Buster trot along happily on his lead. Only once we were all back in the elevator did I allow myself to relax.

'You seem stressed, darling,' Vince murmured. 'I could give you a massage?' he offered. The word 'massage' was laced with suggestion.

I whipped around to face him. 'I'm stressed because someone was murdered in my booth. I'm stressed because I'm supposed to be selling my business and my booth is shut until tomorrow, so I am missing out on countless clients I paid handsomely to meet, and I am stressed because you keep turning up and messing with me.'

'I came to help, darling,' Vince's expression was that of a dog being kicked by its master.

'Stop calling me that. We are not an item. We are not together. We are never going to be together. Please get that through the dense matter you call a brain.' Mindy and Philippe backed away as my ranting took over. 'I have a date tonight and you are not it.'

'Sooo, just some help with the investigation, then,' Vince attempted to clarify.

He just never gave up.

'No, Mr Slater. I do not require your help. I can conduct my own investigation. You should return to your own business.'

The elevator pinged and a moment later the doors swished open. I tugged gently on Buster's lead and set off toward my room, never once looking back to see what Vince might be doing. I just didn't care.

In my room, I put Amber down and unclipped Buster's collar from his lead. Amber jumped onto my bed to stay out of the dog's reach, but Buster was noisily slurping water from his bowl and getting it everywhere.

Amber eyed me critically.

'Yes, it's dinner time,' I answered her unspoken question. She couldn't tell time – the concept was completely lost on both of them – but they knew when it was time for a meal.

I felt tense, which came as no surprise given the events of the day and was questioning what I ought to do to relieve that when a quiet knock at the door disturbed my train of thought.

It also caused Buster to bark, an impulse reaction he seemed unable to avoid. His face was still in his water bowl when he did it, so he created a small tidal wave that threw water up around his ears and all over the floor.

Amber grunted a noise of disgust. *'Dogs.'*

*'It's Mindy,'* Buster announced, wagging his tail. Water dripped off his eyebrows.

'Auntie? Aunt Felicity are you in there?' Mindy called through the door. Of course, she knew I was in my room because she had followed me along the corridor to get to her room next door.

I opened the door and left it that way, crossing my room to the box on the counter containing the pet food and their bowls. Each got a pouch of meaty treats – Liver and rabbit for Buster, Salmon for Amber.

Mindy was hovering in my doorway, waiting for me to give her my attention and for once she looked uncertain.

'Um, are we okay, Auntie?' she asked, a trace of timidity in her tone.

I fixed her with a neutral expression. 'Do you mean am I mad that you set me up on a date with Edward and called Vince the lecherous nightmare when I expressly asked you not to?'

'Um, yes?' Mindy's usual calm demeanour was missing, and she looked off balance without it. Was I going to shout at her? Should I get angry with my teenage assistant for messing with elements of my life that she had no right to even know about?

Truthfully, I considered it. However, a voice at the back of my head reminded me that Mindy had witnessed a man die today and she is only nineteen. We were hardly operating on standard business conditions, and she was right that Vince would answer the call for help and then give it willingly. I dreaded to think what I might be doing now if he hadn't rescued us from Primrose's room.

I let my shoulders droop and hung my head.

'I'm glad you called Vince, okay? I led us into a bad situation, and you willingly followed me. I'm not sure I deserve the trust you give me.' Mindy's smile returned. 'Just don't go setting me up on any more dates, okay?'

I got a thumbs up in response. 'Philippe and I are going for a drink. Do you want to join us? It's been kind of a hectic day.'

She wasn't wrong about that. I shook my head though.

'Thank you, but I think I will get a bath and wash my hair. Thanks to you, I have to make myself look date ready.'

Mindy was good enough to look embarrassed, but said, 'Edward seems really nice.'

I couldn't argue. 'He is really nice.' I felt a kind of maternal need to bring Mindy in and close the door. I wanted to explain to her what it is like to be married to someone for such a long time and then lose them. My husband had been gone long enough now that I could think about him without feeling my heart ache, and I recognised that it was okay to move on if I met someone and wanted to. That all felt like unnecessary effort when I could just pray Mindy never had to experience anything like it herself.

Neither of us had said anything for a few seconds when I heard Philippe's voice echoing along the corridor.

'Are we going, or what, Mindz?' The man could put a zed into anything. 'I needz a mimosa, gurl!'

'You go,' I insisted, grasping the door, and using it to push her out. 'Have fun. I'll see you in the morning.'

'Okay, Auntie.' Mindy hopped back into the corridor. 'I hope your date goes well.'

Phillippe called for her to hurry up again as she jogged out of sight. I closed the door and leaned against it.

'*I need to go outside*,' announced Buster.

'Again?'

Buster tilted his head to one side. '*Food goes in, something has to come out.*'

I shushed him into silence – I did not need a description.

Amber curled up on my bed, her eyes already shut before I got my coat back on. There was a portable travel potty for her in the corner of the bathroom. Cats are so much easier to manage.

Outside, a light drizzle dampened my hair, skin, and clothing. It was that sort of misty rain that looks too insignificant to care about, but clings to your clothing to soak it all the same.

In the heart of London, you might think green spaces would be hard to come by, but the hotel overlooks St James's Park. The landscaped area was perfect for walking a dog or going for a run. There were plenty of people doing one or the other.

At this time of the year, it is dark before teatime and cold even when the sun is up, so I was glad when Buster got on with his 'business' swiftly and I could return to the warmth and get out of the rain. On the way back into the hotel, I bumped into Reed coming out.

A pang of guilt shot through me, irrational because Reed had no idea what I had been up to today. To cover it up, I threw him a wave and a pleasant smile.

'Done for the day?' I enquired.

He nodded, looking weary. 'Yes. It was busier than I expected. Listen, um, sorry,' he stuttered. 'About that business with Mrs Green ...'

'Is she guilty?' I asked, diverting the course of the conversation because I felt certain he was going to ask me about the surprise Primrose found in her handbag.

'Of tampering with the cable?' he clarified. 'Hard to say. The honest answer is that I don't think so. If she is, then Mrs Green is a very good actor. There was nothing to tie her to what happened. I'm not sure anyone is to blame.'

'You're still listing it as an accident then?'

Something caught Reed's eye, his attention shifting away from me to a point behind and to my left. Instinctively, I twisted to see what might have distracted him and found an attractive young woman waiting patiently a few yards away.

She was a natural redhead. Though it was dark out, light from the hotel illuminated the young woman, showing off her lustrous strawberry curls. She had wonderful volume to her hair – a hairdressers dream perhaps.

She had a bright red umbrella above her head that matched her winter coat. Both were made by Karen Millen, a favourite designer of mine and one who hailed from the same county no less. The rain had dampened the young woman's hair, but she didn't seem to care. The sparkle in her eyes as she looked up the hotel steps at Reed told a story – she was in love with him.

Reed brought his attention back to me, but there was a smile teasing the corners of his mouth now – he felt the same about her.

'I'm holding you up,' I acknowledged.

'Not a bit, Mrs Philips. I hope you have a better day tomorrow. I will be keeping a close eye on you – I fear Mrs Green holds a grudge.'

I dipped my head and stepped to the side, my body language telling him to get on with his evening. As he jogged by me and down the steps to the pavement, the young woman tilted her umbrella back so they could kiss, then looped her arm through his.

I watched for a second, reminiscing about being that young and how much in love I had been. Was there still time for me to experience that rush of emotion again? What is it like to find love much later in life? Is it more precious because you understand life more clearly, or does the flame burn less brightly because you are scarred from previous experiences?

It wasn't a subject I planned to put a lot of thought to. I wasn't looking for love. I wasn't looking for anything. I was ... I was entertaining the idea that there might yet be an adventure waiting for me, that's what I was doing.

Pushing the subject to one side, I got out of the rain, smiling my thanks to the doorman as he held the entrance open for me.

I had two hours to get myself ready for a date and the preparation required was going to be mostly mental.

I took my time in the bath, raiding the minifridge for a gin and tonic to enjoy while I soaked away the stress of the day. It absolutely wasn't to calm my nerves because I was going to dinner with a handsome man who was clearly interested in me and that is the story I am sticking to.

Dressed in the outfit I deemed to be my least weddingy – all I brought with me was wedding appropriate clothing and hats/fascinators - I checked my face in the mirror for the twentieth time, looked at the huge pile of discarded outfits on the bed, and promised to pick them all up later.

They had all proven to be too low at the neckline. Not that I wanted to look like a librarian, but showing off some cleavage, which many of my tops and dresses do, did not feel appropriate for dinner with Edward.

The unwarranted nerves I felt continued to increase in the elevator as it descended. If I were not already a long-time friend of Edward's, I would probably run back to my room and lie that I had taken ill. As it was, making my way to the bar, I swear it felt like ascending the steps to the hangman's platform.

I was a few minutes early, but Edward was already there. Sitting by himself at a table for two, there was a single red rose on the placemat opposite his and a bottle of champagne in an ice bucket next to the table.

He was fiddling with his phone, passing the time until I arrived and upon seeing him, I instantly relaxed.

It was Edward. I knew Edward. He was lovely. What on Earth had I been worried about?

He saw me coming and got to his feet.

'Felicity,' he greeted me, and there was an awkward moment when I thought he was going to try to kiss me – too soon, or shake my hand – too formal, so we air kissed as we might on any other occasion.

'Good evening, Edward,' I replied, when we both took a step back to put space between us again. 'Have you been waiting long?'

'No, no, not long. Half an hour maybe. I wanted to make sure they gave us a good table.' He held my chair so I could sit and returned to his side of the table.

'Can I offer you some champagne?' he asked. 'I am drinking scotch; they have an excellent selection here including a 1942 Dalmore. It is so rare to find a bar that will stock such exquisite bottles.' He sensed how much he was talking up his drink of choice and toned it down quickly. 'I love champagne though. I'd be happy to share a bottle with you.'

He was gabbling, filling the air with words and it took me a second to realise he was just as nervous as me.

I reached across the table, to place a hand on top of his.

He looked down at it and then back up at me.

'It was nice of you to offer champagne, Edward. It is not necessary though. Please enjoy your whisky and I'll get myself a gin and tonic when the waiter comes over.'

Edward, like a kindergarten child who knows the answer, shot his hand into the air to draw attention our way. A waiter in an all-black outfit began wending his way through the restaurant.

Hungry because I hadn't eaten much today and worried my stomach might start rumbling, I had my head in the menu when the waiter came to our table.

'A gin and tonic for the lady, please,' instructed Edward.

'Hendricks with slimline tonic and cucumber,' I added without looking up. Whoever was responsible for writing the menu was a master wordsmith, I was getting hungrier with every line.

'And a Dalmore 42. Better make it a single though.'

With the drinks order given, I heard the waiter depart and looked up to meet Edward's gaze once more.

'I'm looking forward to enjoying a pleasant meal. Have you looked at the menu?' I asked. 'The food all sounds exquisite.' There were no prices – it was that kind of place. If you needed to ask how much something was, you couldn't afford it.

Prompted by my question, Edward lifted his own menu.

We discussed the food and waited for another waiter to appear. We were making small talk as one does, discussing weddings and in particular the forthcoming, yet still secret wedding of Prince Markus. When we did so, we kept our voices low because we had both signed a non-disclosure agreement on the subject.

Legally bound to not tell anyone what we knew, we could talk to each other because we were both in the inner circle. It was Edward who tipped me the nod more than a month ago when a palace aide arranged for the prince to buy an engagement ring in his boutique.

The waiter returned with my drink, carefully placing it down in front of me. Edward held up his empty glass and took its full replacement.

We ordered our food, our conversation stalling while we each took a turn instructing the waiter, and then silence ruled as we each thought of something new to talk about.

I sipped at my gin and tonic, loving the crisp clean taste as it washed over my tastebuds. Putting the glass to my mouth acted as an indication that I was not about to start talking and so Edward filled the void.

He talked about his nephew, a young man who was going to graduate from Oxford next year with a double first. His younger brother's eldest son was then set to join Edward at the family business. With no children of his own – Edward admitted never meeting the right woman, and locked eyes with me when he did so – he was glad there was a new generation of the family coming to work with him.

There was an intensity to Edward's stare, and it caused me to feel just a little uncomfortable. A voice in the back of my head told me it was exactly the same way that Vince always looked at me. I banished the voice and told it to stay quiet – I did not like Vince.

*He has a nice body*. The voice reminded me, providing an image of Vince without his clothes on.

'Oh shuttup.' I snapped

'I'm sorry?' Edward had a confused and concerned look on his face.

Arguing with the voice in my head, who kept reminding me of Vince's positive attributes in the most annoying fashion, I had unintentionally spoken out loud.

'Oh, nothing,' I mumbled. 'You were telling me about your nephew,' I reminded him although technically that wasn't true.

'No, Felicity,' Edward reached across the table to take my hand. 'I was telling you how I had never met the right woman … until now.'

The intense look was back.

I swallowed hard. He wasn't gripping my hand – I could pull it free if I wanted to, yet as my panic began to simmer, I could not decide what the right thing to do might be.

'We have known each other a long time, Felicity,' he reminded me, his intense gaze boring into my head. 'Long enough that I believe I know you as a person. You are professional and determined. You possess a keen intelligence and a strong sense of business acumen.'

This was all very nice – getting complimented and all, but where was he going with it and why were all his compliments to do with my work?

He continued, 'You are kind and giving. You are elegant and utterly gorgeous.'

Ok, this was better, but now he was going a little over the top.

'Water for the table, sir?' asked a waiter, arriving with a pitcher of iced water.

Something about the waiter's voice made me want to look up and see who it was. I knew the voice from somewhere, but I could not manage to shift my gaze from Edward's.

Edward's face twitched in annoyance. 'Later,' he snapped irritably, his eyes never leaving mine. 'I was so glad that you agreed to meet me for dinner today, Felicity.'

Edward was twitching in his seat. He was nervous about something, though I had no idea what.

'I'll just put it down so you can help yourselves,' said the waiter.

Edward still had hold of my right hand with his left but was reaching into his inner jacket pocket with his right. Like a hammer striking my skull, my brain suddenly worked out what was going on and why Edward was so nervous.

My heart chose to take a well-deserved work break at that point. It didn't fail or explode, it simply chose to stop beating because I knew what was about to happen and couldn't get any part of my body to operate.

'Aaaaaahh!' cried the waiter, clumsily setting the pitcher of water down at an angle so it tipped and fell.

Just as Edward was pulling something from his jacket pocket, a flood of icy cold water shot across his half of the table and into his lap.

Edward jolted, trying to evade the terrible wave, but ultimately found himself pinned in place by the waiter who had inexplicably moved behind Edward so he couldn't scoot his chair back to escape.

'Waaaah!' yelled Edward as the ice and water poured into his lap.

'Oh, goodness!' exclaimed the waiter.

I was on my feet, reacting to the terrible accident when my eyes twitched up to find the waiter grinning.

I couldn't believe my eyes. 'Vince!'

Vince stepped back so that Edward could finally get out of his chair, but the damage was done now.

'I'm so terribly sorry,' lied Vince. He was dressed as a waiter. He even had one of the hotel's waistcoats on. Using the small towel that had been folded over his arm, Vince was dabbing at Edward's groin. He wasn't doing it gently.

Edward swiped at Vince's arm, parrying it way. 'What the devil is going on?' he demanded to know. 'Get off me, you utter oaf!'

Vince darted back a pace, unable to suppress a giggle.

'I shall be speaking with your manager!' raged the jeweller.

I was on my feet, glaring across the table. Vince saw my expression and let his smile fall.

'What?' he asked, challenging me to unleash on him if I dared. 'I just rescued you again, Felicity. This bozo was about to propose. Who even is he?'

'Edward is an old friend,' I growled. 'He and I were just having dinner.'

Edward's attention had been on his soaking groin until Vince started talking. Now his eyes were flicking between the 'waiter' and me, confusion darkening his features.

'You two know each other?' Edward demanded to know.

Vince clapped him on the shoulder. 'Sorry, old boy. Felicity and I are an item.'

'We are not an item!' I roared, picking up a fork from the table and wondering if this would count as justifiable homicide.

'She says that all the time,' laughed Vince. 'She is such a tease.' Making his face serious for a moment, Vince said, 'Sorry about the iced water all over the family jewels there, old boy. But … don't go trying to steal another man's woman,' he finished with a shrug.

The head waiter arrived.

'What is going on here?' he addressed Vince, then got a look at his face. 'Wait, who are you?'

Vince nodded his head in my direction. 'This lady's boyfriend.'

I stabbed the fork into the table with enough force that it stuck there.

Vince was still talking. 'One accepts a certain amount of interest from other parties when one attempts to capture such a great prize.' Vince was taking off his jacket and tie. 'Here,' he said, handing them to the head waiter. 'I 'borrowed' these.'

Ignoring Vince and the head waiter, plus all the people in the restaurant looking our way, Edward focused his attention on me.

'I'm sorry, Felicity. I wish you had said you were already involved with someone,' he put the ring box back into his jacket pocket. 'I have misjudged my position.' With a final nod of his head, he turned on his heel and strode away through the restaurant.

'Edward,' I called after him. I wanted to explain that Vince was nothing more than an insufferable idiot who needed a damned good smack in the trousers. We were not together, and we never would be, but Edward was already too far away for me to explain any of that. Not without shouting, and the restaurant's patrons had already suffered enough interruptions.

Edward had intended to propose. I'd seen him reaching into his jacket pocket and knew what he was going to produce long before I saw it. Vince knew it too and … what? He'd been tailing me? He knew I had a date tonight because Philippe told him earlier. I thought Vince left after I dismissed him earlier, but he hadn't, he chose to hang around so he could ruin things.

Or had he saved me again? It wasn't as if I was going to say yes to Edward. With thoughts spinning and colliding in my head, I knew I would have turned Edward down. Yes, we had known each other for years, but what was he thinking pulling out a ring?

I would have told him no, but I would have dated him afterwards. Like Vince, he was open about his interest in me. Unlike Vince he wasn't a horrible rogue with a shark-infested smile.

Edward made it to the restaurant doors and exited without once looking back.

'Annnnd … good riddance,' Vince turned to me, clapping his hands with glee. 'Shall we eat, darling?' he enquired politely. 'What did Edward order? I could just have that. Was it a nice, juicy steak?'

The head waiter, bewildered by events, finally had a question he could answer.

'The gentleman ordered the seabass in a passionfruit glaze with lime foam and beetroot compote.'

Vince screwed his face up. 'Goodness. I really did save you, Felicity.'

Ignoring him, and trying to keep my anger in check, I addressed the head waiter.

'Please send the bill for the food and drinks to my room.' Taking care to never once look Vince's way, I picked up my handbag, a small clutch that went with my outfit, not the gaudy, awful Flirkin thing I bought earlier, and I, too, made my way to the exit.

Falling into step at my shoulder, Vince said, 'Skipping the main course and heading straight for the Vince souffle for dessert, eh?'

Just before I got to the doors, I stopped walking and spun on my heels to face him.

'If you follow me, I will call for security. If you touch me, I will scream. If you somehow turn up somewhere I don't expect you to be, I will call the police and report you as a stalker. I do not expect to see you ever again, Vince Slater.'

I twisted back to face the door, thought better of it, and spun around again, swinging my right hand to slap his face. I could not remember when I last hit someone, but as my palm stung, and I walked away with a chorus of cheers from several women in the restaurant, I could not help but note Vince had made no attempt to block my strike.

## Confrontation

Leaving the restaurant, I spotted Melissa leaving the event hall. It was late for her to still be working, and I found myself questioning how many hours she might have put in today. What was it that was so important at this time of the evening that she had to attend to it herself? I felt certain I would have found a way to delegate it.

In the elevator on my way to my room, hungry because I missed dinner, I tussled with what to say to Edward and whether I should go to his room. If I convinced him that Vince was nothing but a nightmare suitor I wanted to be rid of, would he believe me? If he did, would the ring then reappear?

It was all too much to figure out and my day had been long and exhausting.

I ordered room service, the same meal I was supposed to have in the restaurant, so thanks to Vince I ended up paying a small fortune for just one dinner which I had to eat with my cat and dog like some kind of lonely spinster. I also raided the minibar again, working my way through over half of its contents as I fumed and ground my teeth together.

I was still fuming when I woke up the next morning. Wisely perhaps, Vince had not chosen to message me with an apology. Had he done so, my reply might have been quite short.

Showered and dressed, I took Buster for a walk before breakfast.

The sun was not yet up, and the air was cold under clear skies as we walked beneath the streetlights of St James's Park. Buster chased a squirrel. Actually, he attempted to chase several but each time he did it was like watching a race between a Formula One car and a cheeseburger.

Since he was never going to catch one, I let him get on with it, listening to the angry squirrels chittering their displeasure from the safety of the branches above.

While he snuffled in the undergrowth, I thought about the previous day and questioned whether I might, in fact, owe Primrose an apology. She wasn't going to get one, but a lot of yesterday had been about attempting to prove she was guilty of murder. Though it loathed me to admit it, it looked as though she was more than likely innocent.

Had it just been a terrible accident then?

The wedding fayre was due to reopen at ten, which gave me three hours. There had been no damage to my booth that I was aware of. Nevertheless, I wanted to get in to inspect it and make sure it was set and ready before I went for breakfast.

Certain Amber was fine to be left on her own in my room, I turned right when I got back to the hotel and walked directly through to the venue.

Imagine my surprise when I found Mindy there already.

'Am I all right like this?' she asked, indicating her clothes.

I insist upon wedding attire at all times when we are working – skirts or dresses, jackets if it is cool and either hats or fascinators. We are selling fantasy weddings and need to look the part. Mindy habitually wore sportswear or, as she put it, clothes she could move in.

My niece is athletic and strong, lithe rather than muscular, but above all she is a nimble little minx and complains that no one can fight in a fitted skirt. I felt sure that was true and had once seen her hitch a skirt up to her waist so she could surprise a man with her panty-clad lower half.

She then demonstrated her martial arts prowess by kicking him in the side of his head.

I took in her fitness attire and let it pass. It would be hours before the rush of potential clients began to fill the hall.

'Is there much left to do?' I asked.

Mindy looked around. 'Not really, Auntie. I dusted and vacuumed and made sure everything is straight. One of the hotel maintenance guys fixed the cable for the refrigerator so our drinks are cold and ready to go. We have plenty of brochures and leaflets to hand out.' She looked about again. 'Is there anything I missed?'

I gave myself a few seconds of thinking time, but concluded, 'No, I don't think so. Well done, Mindy. Thank you for being so proactive.'

Mindy grinned and Buster wagged his tail.

'Breakfast?' I enquired.

'*Sounds good,*' said Buster.

'If there's time, I'd like to get in a workout?' suggested Mindy cautiously.

How could I possibly say no? It wasn't as if I needed her to do anything else – she'd already done it all. Asking her to be back at half past nine for a final run through and to catch up with Justin, who already messaged to let me know he was in bound, I watched her jog away.

She was off to the gym, somewhere I probably ought to go myself. Telling myself I couldn't because unfortunately I 'forgot' to pack any gym gear, I tugged at Buster's lead and started back toward the hotel lobby.

Primrose stepped into my path. She did not look happy to see me.

'I lost almost the whole day yesterday, Flicky,' she grumbled angrily. 'The stupid hotel security idiots wanted to go through my things. Do you know what it's like to have half a dozen men rooting through your underwear?'

I couldn't help but smirk at her choice of words and only just managed to refrain from saying, 'I always thought you were that type of woman.'

The flash of mirth crossing my face proved to be incendiary.

'You put poop in my handbag!' she shouted, her arms twitching as she fought to contain her rage.

Feigning innocence and trying not to enjoy myself too much – honestly I was – I replied, 'Someone put poop in your handbag? Is that the one you accused me of stealing? Remind me again where it was found.'

Primrose took a step toward me, pausing only when Buster emitted a low growl.

'That dog,' she pointed an accusing finger. 'It was from that dog, wasn't it?' She forced a smile. 'Well, I'm going to have the last laugh, Felicity. I sent the poop to be analysed. I'm going to prove you did it and then everyone will hear about you and your 'dirty' tricks.'

Not bothering to suppress my grin any longer, I said, 'But you don't have it, Primrose. Reed took it from you and disposed of it.'

Primrose stopped instantly as her brain processed my words. 'How could you possibly know that?' she asked.

My cheeks coloured and I swore inside my head.

Her gasp of realisation was something to behold. 'You *were* in my room!' she shrieked. 'You heard the whole conversation. Guards! Guards!'

There were no hotel security guards in sight. Nor were there any in earshot because no one came to see what the fuss was about. A few stallholders poked their heads out, saw that it was Primrose shouting again, and went back to what they were doing.

Quivering, Primrose levelled an index finger at me. 'I am going to get you, Felicity Philips. Just you mark my words.'

'Is that a threat?' I enquired with the tone of someone checking their coffee has been sweetened.

Primrose made to stride past me, but Buster blocked her way and barked when she came near.

'That beast needs to be put down,' she growled, taking a different route to get around me.

I let her go, breathing a sigh of relief that she had no evidence I had done anything. If she possessed one jot of it, she would already be calling the police, the FBI, and quite possibly the A-Team.

I let go a huff of air, refilled my lungs, and started toward the hotel lobby again. It was breakfast time.

Justin found me at breakfast, settling into the chair opposite to join me. He asked about what Mindy and I got up to the previous day and whether I had found somewhere nice for dinner.

I elected to be lean with the details – he didn't need to hear about handbags full of poop, ruined dates with world class jewellers, or stupid private investigators. There had still been no contact from Vince, and I was beginning to believe he might have finally got the message.

The sensation of being watched stole over me, making my skin crawl. When I snapped my head around to find Vince, I made Justin jump.

'Goodness, Felicity. Is everything all right?' he asked.

There was no sign of Vince though I continued to glare across the room at the spot I thought he might be hiding. Could he really still be here? What was it going to take to make him get the message?

'Felicity?' Justin called my name again, this time prompting a response.

'Sorry,' I turned back to face him. 'I am jumping at shadows.'

On the far side of the restaurant, Edward followed a waitress to an empty table. On any other occasion, he would have sought me out to say hello. Not today though and that was all down to Vince. Now that we had both been able to sleep on it, I felt a need to address the issue of last night. I wasn't going to mention the ring box, but I did need to apologise for Vince's behaviour.

'Would you excuse me for a moment?' I asked.

I got to my feet, but before I could start moving, Melissa, the event organiser and hotel deputy manager came to Edward's table. She didn't sit down, but she was talking to him about something and her relaxed posture – rather than poised to get moving again – suggested she might be there for a while.

I settled back into my chair just as my breakfast arrived and when I next looked his way, Edward was nowhere to be seen. He was avoiding me, and even though I had done nothing wrong, I was going to have to be the one to do all the work.

With our meals eaten, Justin went to the event hall while I returned to my room to check on Amber and Buster. They had eaten, they had water, and could probably be relied upon to sleep for the next few hours. Mindy would take them both out at lunchtime and guest services knew to leave my room alone – this was not my first time here with animals.

With that task complete and the second day of the wedding fayre due to start in an hour, I returned to the hall. There was most likely nothing for me to do there until the visitors began to arrive, but I liked to give myself time to relax and prepare for the onslaught.

I was busy trying to get the flowers to sit right in the vase again when I heard feet come to a stop behind me.

'Good morning, Felicity.'

I was shocked to hear Edward's voice. He had chosen to seek me out rather than the other way around. Still mortified by the previous evening, I started speaking before I was even facing him.

'Edward I am so sorry about what happened last night. Vince and I are nothing more than acquaintances, you have to believe me.' The sincerity of my claim looked to surprise him, and I came forward to take his hands in mine. 'Vince is a private detective. I met him during that awful incident at Loxton Hall.'

106

'But you are involved?' Edward was frowning, wanting to believe me but uncertain that he should.

I shook my head vigorously. 'Not in any way, nor have we ever been. Vince clearly wants to be, but I have never given him the slightest indication that I am interested.'

Edward considered my claim for a moment.

'Where is he now?'

'I have no idea and I do not care. I made it very clear that I would call the police and accuse him of stalking me if I saw him again.' Edward didn't reply, keeping his thoughts to himself and giving nothing away. It left me feeling awkward and as if I needed to say something. 'Can we try our date again?' I enquired.

Edward didn't answer my question, but he did respond, letting go of my left hand and reaching inside his jacket with his right just as he had last night. 'I want to clear something up, Felicity. Something I believe you misconstrued, and I had no chance to clarify last night.'

Watching his hand as he withdrew it again with the ring box once again in his grasp, I said, 'Go on.'

Edward looked down at the box, and with it facing him, flicked it open using just the thumb of the hand which held it. I guess master jewellers learn to do stuff like that.

'This is not an engagement ring,' he assured me. 'And I was not going to propose last night. That we might one day become more than friends has been a thought in the back of my head for several years.'

He didn't say ever since my husband died, but I was sure that was what he meant. I let it pass.

He turned the ring box around, revealing a gold cameo ring inset with diamonds.

'I came across this many years ago and have been holding onto it ever since with the hope that I might one day find a person to wear it for me.'

I could feel my heartbeat getting faster. The ring was beautiful. Expertly handcrafted, the carved face was …

'Wait,' I blurted, 'isn't that …'

'Queen Victoria? Yes, Felicity.'

I wasn't going to ask, but my guess would be that the ring was worth a small fortune. The sort of piece that could be swapped for a house.

'Are you all set up?' asked Reed, arriving from behind Edward and clearly not noticing that we were caught in a moment.

Edward kept hold of my left hand as he turned to face the head of security. It made me feel a little awkward, but I chose not to fight it.

'I hope you have a more successful day of it, Mrs Philips,' Mr Reed offered me a hopeful smile.

'Thank you, Mr Reed,' I nodded my head.

He chuckled for some reason. 'It's just Reed,' he corrected me. I had his name wrong and had called him Mr Reed half a dozen times or more. 'Did they fix that cable? I sent the maintenance crew to make sure it was all safe before we put the power back on.'

Mindy was coming through doors to the hall behind him, her fitness clothes swapped out for a floral print summer dress and tall wedge heels. I got a wave from her as she ducked around Reed's back and went into our booth to talk to Justin. She held my gaze long enough to flare her eyes because I was standing next to the man I went on a date with last night and we were holding hands.

She would have subtle questions about that later which would grow less subtle the longer I refused to answer.

To Edward, I hissed, 'Can you give me a few seconds.' At a more normal volume, and with my arm up to invite Reed inside, I pointed toward the back of the booth, saying, 'Let's take a look, shall we?'

I was content that the repair would be complete – Mindy already told me it was, but it made sense to check it.

The cable was not, in fact repaired, whoever came to attend to the task swapped out the original cable for a completely new one. Reed inspected their handiwork and nodded his approval.

'I shall let you get on with your day, Mrs Philips. Please let me know if you have any trouble from … um …'

'Primrose Green?' asked Mindy, eavesdropping on our conversation. 'She's been watching our booth for the last ten minutes, Auntie. She's up to something, you can bet on it.'

'Why?' asked Justin. 'What happened yesterday? Did I miss something?'

As we all swung our collective gaze across the hall to where Mindy indicated, Primrose ducked her head back behind the edge of a stall.

Reed harrumphed, setting his jaw. 'I think perhaps I should have a word with her.' He wasted no time, marching away from us to make sure my rival wasn't going to do anything rash.

I think we all heard the sound at the same time, though none of us knew what it was. I looked up, my eyes drawn above my head to stare up at the ceiling and that was when I saw what had made the noise.

Frozen to the spot in fear, my feet refusing to obey the simplest of commands, I sensed everyone else getting out of the way.

A lighting gantry, made from steel and suspended from the internal structure of the event hall had broken free and was gladly obeying gravity on its way back to earth. I had no idea what it might weigh, but significantly more than me was an accurate enough answer given the situation and how long it appeared that I had to live.

Reed was walking away, heading toward Primrose and already too far from me to help. Mindy had thrown herself to the side, no doubt expecting me to do the same. Edward was five yards away, waiting patiently for me to return to him and Justin was running for cover and not looking back. Only yours truly was too dumb to get out of the way of the steel beam free falling toward her head.

I heard shouts, terrified voices telling me to jump out of the way, but I had paused for too long and there was too little time for me to escape getting crushed.

Was this a good time to close my eyes? Would Mindy look after Amber and Buster?

All the breath in my lungs left in one great whoosh as something slammed into me from the side a nanosecond before the lighting gantry crashed down through the spot I had occupied.

I heard gasps of shock, and squeals of surprise, plus a terrifying grunt of pain.

I hit the ground completely out of control, bruising the entire left side of my body and whacking my head on the floor. It might be covered in carpet, but it felt like stone anyway. There was someone with me I realised, their arms tangled with my legs as we came to a stop.

The world was full of running feet all coming my way, the sound of the lighting gantry coming to a rest, and alarmed shouts as multiple individuals all tried to take control of the situation at the same time.

Hands hooked under my arms, pulling me to the side to get away from where I landed to some supposed safety a few feet away. My ribs were killing me and taking a breath hurt, but as Mindy and others got in my face, attempting to ascertain if I was injured or not, my only thought was for the person who saved me.

Someone crashed into me right before the steel thing would have killed me and I heard their grunt of pain when the falling object hit them instead. Between the legs of those who had rushed to help, I could see an outstretched arm on the floor. It wasn't moving.

Who had taken my place? Had they sacrificed themself to save me?

Holding my ribs, I shoved against Mindy to get a better look and saw my saviour's face.

It was Vince.

I groaned and let my desire to lie down win.

'Primrose. It was Primrose,' insisted Mindy. She was highly agitated and arguably one of the deadliest people in the hall. She wanted to ask Mrs Green some 'questions'. By which she probably meant knock her out, tie her up, and apply methods of questioning not employed since the dark ages.

'We don't know that,' argued Reed.

I was sitting up and massaging some of my bruised areas. Justin brought me a chair from one of the tables in our booth and, together with Mindy, helped me up and into it.

'She threatened to get even with me,' I told the head of hotel security while wincing from the effort.

'And she was watching,' added Mindy triumphantly as if it were all the additional evidence required.

A minute had passed since the heavy light fitting miraculously detached from the ceiling and fell to earth. I was too woozy from shock to get to my feet, but I badly wanted to check on Vince.

'Is he okay?' I begged to know. 'Mindy, can you see if he is badly hurt?'

Mindy left my side to do as I asked. The press of people around him were being corralled by members of Reed's security team and making space for first aiders to get to him. Mindy forced her way close enough to see, and as she squeezed in to look over the head of a shorter person, I saw that it was Melissa, the event organiser.

'I saw the whole thing,' she revealed as she came to check on me. 'What he did was so brave. Do you know who he is?'

'Is he hurt?' I asked, rudely ignoring her question.

A little startled by the passion in my words, Melissa glanced back at the stricken P.I. before mumbling, 'He's out cold and there is a nasty lump on his skull. I don't think anything is broken though.'

He caught a heavy piece of falling steel with his head. Was his brain going to be okay? I knew concussion was not to be taken lightly, so he might look to be in one piece, but it could be hours or days before we knew for sure. What if he was in a coma?

The chilling thought stole through my body, making me feel cold, and then immensely relieved when we all heard Vince come around.

He coughed and winced and mumbled something I couldn't catch. Still worried my legs might not support me if I tried to get up, I continued to peer at Vince through the gaps in the crowd. That is until someone deliberately chose to block my view.

'You told me he went home, Felicity.' I looked up to find Edward frowning down at me. He hadn't snarled his words, if anything they came out devoid of emotion, but when he spoke again, there was no mistaking how disappointed with me he was. 'Did the two of you spend the night together laughing about me?'

I was horrified by his question. 'No, Edward! How could you think such a thing?'

The jeweller pursed his lips and crossed his arms. 'I do not like being made to feel foolish, Felicity. I shall, of course, maintain our business relationship, but I think it best if we curtail any future thoughts of social interaction.'

I opened my mouth to yet again protest my innocence, but Edward was already gone, weaving through the crowd to get away.

Justin leaned down to whisper next to my ear. 'He didn't even ask if you were okay, Felicity.'

It was a valid point, but I would forgive Edward for his actions in the heat of the moment. None of this was his fault and he had every right to feel betrayed and suspicious.

'Can you help me up?' I begged, raising my right arm so Justin could assist me to stand.

Melissa had moved away, catching hold of Reed so she could talk to him. Between them, they needed to come to a decision about what to do now. The event was due to open in half an hour and there would be people staying at the hotel just to make attending the wedding show easier. On top of that, there would be thousands of people coming to visit from all over the country and, in some cases, farther afield.

Could they open? Was it safe?

Paramedics arrived, jogging into the hall from the direction of the hotel lobby, each carrying a heavy bag full of equipment, dressings, and goodness knows what else. Right behind them were men in overalls – the hotel maintenance crew.

My only interest was in Vince. Whatever else I thought about him, he had just saved my life.

Now that I was up and on my feet, I found I could stand without needing Justin's support. I let go of him, but he came with me as I advanced on the paramedics. There was a two-yard bubble around Vince who was still on the floor and making no attempt to get up. Reed's guys were keeping everyone back but now the initial flurry of excitement had passed, those here to sell their wares or services were either drifting back to their booths or haranguing Melissa out of concern the event might be closed for the day.

I heard people arguing that their stand was over the other side of the hall and therefore nowhere near the scene of yesterday and today's drama. Others were getting angry and demanding a by-the-hour refund if the hall did not open on time.

I tuned them out as the paramedics told Vince he was concussed and needed to go to hospital.

'Are you okay, Auntie?' Mindy wanted to know, appearing by my side. 'Primrose is in her stand pretending she had nothing to do with what just happened. Everyone else came over to see when the gantry fell, but she went the other way.'

Mindy was ready to find Primrose guilty and move straight on to sentencing. I felt much the same but could not for the life of me imagine how Primrose got the heavy light fitting to fall.

'The bolts are undone,' declared one of the maintenance guys. They were off to our left side, inspecting the heavy piece of steel and the lights fitted to it. 'When it fell, it tore the cable free.'

'We'll have to get up there and terminate the wire before it causes another short,' said his colleague.

'Was it loosened?' asked Reed. 'Or never done up properly in the first place?'

The two maintenance guys acted as if it was an accusation.

'Hey, don't look at us,' one protested.

'Yeah, we didn't build it. The firm who built the event hall are the ones you want.' pointed out the other.

Reed shushed them until they were ready to listen. 'No one is suggesting you had anything to do with it, chaps. I am asking if you think someone tampered with it deliberately.'

The two maintenance chaps looked inward at each other, one scratching his chin while the other pulled an uncertain expression.

'Hard to say,' they agreed.

I wanted to quiz them more and find out what a person would need in order to 'cause' this latest accident, but the paramedics had Vince on a stretcher and were preparing to leave. I hadn't heard him speak yet and needed to thank him for saving me – again – before he left.

I detached myself from Reed, Mindy, and the others to pursue the annoying private investigator.

'Vince,' I called. 'Vince, can you hear me?'

His head was held in place with a strap over his forehead and a support that went around his neck, but he twisted slightly to get a better look at me anyway.

'Stay still,' instructed the paramedic at the head end of the stretcher.

'Is that you, Felicity?' he asked.

I put my hand out to touch his arm as the paramedics wheeled him through the hall.

'What are you doing here, Vince? Why didn't you leave last night?'

He didn't reply straight away, and I thought he wasn't going to reply when he mumbled something too quietly for me to hear.

'I'm sorry, Vince. What was that?'

He sighed and spoke more clearly. 'Because I'm in love with you, Felicity.'

My feet stopped moving, the stretcher being pushed along by the two paramedics leaving me behind so I had to run a pace to catch up again.

'No, you are not, Vince,' I argued. 'Why would you say that?'

'Because it's true.' The stretcher's wheels went over the door sill to get outside to the waiting ambulance and in so doing bumped him. Vince winced but carried on talking. 'I have been since I first met you. I've never felt like this about a woman before.'

I couldn't think of anything to say.

The paramedic at the head end of the stretcher said, 'You shouldn't talk. Concussion can make us say things we wouldn't otherwise reveal.

'Shhh!' I insisted. I needed to hear what Vince had to say. 'If any of that is true Vince, why have you been such an annoyingly, awful pain in my backside? Why couldn't you just send me flowers and romance me like anyone else might?'

He tried to shrug – all but impossible with the movement-restricting collar around his neck.

'You make me nervous,' he admitted. 'I get butterflies in my stomach when I see you and I can't seem to make my tongue work properly to say the things I want to say.'

'Seriously, man,' coached the paramedic. 'I've seen this before. Concussed people reveal all their secrets, and they always regret it afterwards. We had this one guy a while ago, he started listing all the things he'd ever done that he regretted and right in front of his wife, he admitted …'

I hushed the man again, shutting him up with a look that threatened castration if he interrupted Vince again.

Doing my best to meet Vince's eyes, I said, 'But you've spied on me, turned up places when you had no right to be there, and you keep trying to get me into bed.'

Vince tapped the paramedic's arm. 'Can you blame me?' he wanted to know.

Wisely, the paramedic didn't answer – I was old enough to be his mother.

Getting no response, Vince flicked his eyes across to look at me. 'I'm sorry,' he mumbled. 'I'm not usually like that. Like I said, I'm not really me when I am around you.'

We reached the back of the ambulance.

'Are you coming with us?' asked the paramedic with the opinion about what not to say when concussed. 'It seems you two have some things to talk about.'

I stared at him for a second, my emotions and pretty much all the rest of me, utterly confused by Vince's revelation. Vince had been driving me nuts for the last few weeks because he was in love with me. That was what he wanted me to believe. Was it true? Or was this another ploy to get me into bed? How could I know the difference? How did I feel about it either way?

There was a definite pull towards him. He was charismatic and handsome. He had a good body, his own career, and lots of other plus points. If he were a car I was thinking about buying, there would be lots of entries in the pro column. However, in the con column was his ability to make me want to boil him in vinegar.

They were loading him into the back of the ambulance, and I needed to make a decision. In the end, it was easy.

I clambered inside so I could look down into his eyes.

'Thank you for saving me, Vince. Call me when you are recovered.' I did not hang around to have a discussion on the subject but waited for the ambulance to depart before heading back inside.

I wanted to go with Vince, not because I was romantically interested in him – the jury needed weeks of deliberation to reach a decision on that one – but because he had come to my rescue several times now and I felt I owed him … something.

Ultimately, though, he got injured in the second 'accident' in two days and I believed neither one of them was any such thing. I almost died in both incidents, and both happened at my booth. There was coincidence and then there was whatever was happening here.

Primrose threatened to get even, and I believed she meant to increase her chances of getting the royal wedding by killing her biggest rival – me.

Now I was going all out to prove it.

The crowd around my booth had thinned by the time I returned, but not by much. I spotted Justin and went to him.

'Are you okay?' I enquired.

He gave me a shocked look and choked out a laugh.

'Am I okay? Are you okay, Felicity? I'm fine. I'm not the one who almost got killed by a lighting gantry.'

I shrugged. The truth was that Vince's confession of love was throwing me more than my second near-fatal accident in twenty-four hours. However, I wasn't telling anyone what Vince said.

Ever, probably.

I was about to say something, when Melissa raised her voice to get everyone's attention. She was surrounded by a horde of concerned vendors, most of whom were pressing her for answers.

'We are going to open the wedding fayre,' she shouted to be heard. 'This was just an accident, and I can assure you there will be a full enquiry. There will be a one-hour delay and I need all of you to vacate the event hall so the maintenance team can inspect the structure. We all need to be sure it is safe.'

She got a fresh barrage of questions in reply. When they began to dwindle, she raised her hands and held them up until the chatter dropped enough for her to speak.

'Please all now follow our head of security, Reed Cartwright, to the exit. Free hot and cold beverages will be laid on in the Chambray conference room on the first floor for anyone who needs somewhere to wait.'

I blinked a couple of times, checking what I just heard and comparing it to what I knew.

'Please, everyone,' Melissa raised her voice a little louder. 'The longer it takes us to get started, the longer it will be before we can open the doors. We must inspect the structure before business can commence today.'

With a goodly amount of griping and groaning, the teams of wedding dress makers, cake bakers, car hire firms, the man with the swans, and everyone else began to make their way toward the doors.

By my side, Justin announced his intention to use the time to work on our proposal for the royal wedding. It was something he and I had just started to look at and there was a lot of work to do if we planned to wow the pants off the prince and his fiancée. Justin left me, hurrying to the doors so he could find a quiet space to work.

'What do we do, Auntie?' whispered Mindy. I had neither seen nor heard her approach, but she was at my shoulder now. 'Do we follow Primrose? Or do we hide here until everyone has gone and see what we can find in her booth?'

'It wasn't her,' I murmured, unable to take my eyes off the event coordinator.

Mindy frowned in her misunderstanding.

'It wasn't Primrose,' I repeated, my eyes still examining the hotel's deputy manager. Melissa's husband was having an affair with a younger, prettier woman and she knew about it. All the little bits of detail from this incident and the last started to line up.

I'd been calling him Mr Reed since I met him, but Reed wasn't his last name, it was his first. His last name was Cartwright, and he was married to Melissa.

Melissa was right by my booth mere seconds before the fatal electrocution yesterday. Then today she appeared seconds after the lighting gantry fell so must have been close by. That put her in the right vicinity on both occasions. Not only that, Reed had been close by too. Today he only moved out of the danger zone because Mindy spotted Primrose spying on us and he felt he could stave off any problems by speaking to her before she did something. Yesterday, he was passing the booth when it happened. He could have so easily touched the poor man who died or touched the frame of my booth. Either thing would have probably killed him.

Melissa knew about the affair – how could she not? Reed was so brazen he had the redhead come to the hotel to meet him after work. Was he leaving Melissa?

If I was right, then Melissa was targeting her husband, the person who wronged her, not the woman he was cheating with. She had motive and opportunity. As hotel manager she could have easily got in here last night and used a maintenance tower to get up high. Had she erected a clever pin or something that she could pull on a wire to send the lighting gantry crashing down?

I nodded my head. The detail of it didn't matter. I was staring at a killer and no one else had any idea.

Now how the heck was I going to prove it?

As everyone filtered out from the event hall, I went with them, taking Mindy with me. I hadn't yet had time to fill her in on the crazy theory swirling like a maelstrom in my head which was why she was arguing with me.

'I'm confused, Auntie. Why aren't we going after Mrs Green? She must be behind this. Surely, she was watching so she would be able to see you get crushed under that lighting gantry when it fell.'

I grabbed her hand and yanked her after me as I went with the crowd.

'I'll explain in a minute,' I promised.

Ten minutes later, Mindy was sitting on my bed stroking Amber's fur while I paced the room trying to get everything straight.

'Melissa wanted everyone out of the event hall so she could personally oversee the removal of the lighting gantry. She must have rigged it so it would fall on her command. There must be a wire or something which she pulled to make it fall at the right moment. It's just like yesterday,' I was piecing it together as I went. 'She's the event organiser so she goes wherever she wants, and no one would ever question it. She was behind our booth right before that poor man got electrocuted.'

'And you think she is trying to kill her husband?' questioned Mindy, a doubtful expression ruling her face. 'Why would she want to do that?' She raised a hand to stop me from answering straight away. 'Not that I don't get it. Don't get me wrong, I want to kill most of the boys I meet. I can only imagine what a few years of being married to one might be like.'

Amber sighed. '*Humans are so weird*,' she remarked.

Buster nodded his head. '*True dat.*'

'*True dat?*' Amber turned her head to look at the dog.

123

Buster put on his rasping, deep Devil Dog voice. '*Yeah, Devil Dog is gangsta, cat. Get used to it.*'

Mindy flicked her eyes between the cat and the dog and then up at me. 'Are they saying something?' she asked.

'Yes, but mostly they are being unkind to humans or just being ridiculous.'

Amber showed me a surprised face. '*How am I being ridiculous? He's the one with the psychotic alter ego. You don't hear me begging for a skateboard with a 50. cal on the front.*'

'*That would have totally completed my image,*' argued Buster. '*It needed spinners on the wheels though.*'

Amber looked down at the dog, thought about arguing, but decided the only sensible option was to go back to sleep.

'As I was saying, Melissa wants to kill her husband. The reason why ...' I told my niece about the redhead I saw him with last night and how they were very obviously involved.

'Men are such pigs,' she grumbled. It terrified me slightly that at nineteen she already had enough experience of the opposite sex to have such a strong opinion.

'The point, really, is that I don't think anyone else is going to figure this out.'

'*Tell the police,*' suggested Amber without even bothering to open her eyes.

Buster had a different plan. '*Deploy Devil Dog,*' he rasped. '*Hey, that was three D's,*' he observed as if it were something special to celebrate.

'I don't have anything to tell the police,' I admitted. 'If I go to them now, they will look at me like I am nuts.'

'*Deploy Devil Dog*,' whispered Buster so quietly it was like hearing a voice inside my head.

Mindy stopped stroking Amber and stretched her arms behind her on the bed so she was looking up at the ceiling but not actually lying down.

'Okay,' she started. 'We need to prove that Melissa is behind the two accidents, right?'

'Right,' I agreed.

'But to do that, we probably need to get our hands on the gantry thing that fell or get up into the structure of the event hall to see if there is evidence of someone tampering with it. And we need to find the original cable from our refrigerator, yes?'

'That would be helpful,' I agreed. It had only recently occurred to me how convenient it was that the original cable had been completely replaced. If Melissa succeeded in killing Reed for his infidelity, and a police enquiry followed, it was far better for there to be no evidence to inspect.

'But we can't get into the event hall right now,' Mindy continued, 'because the person we suspect of causing the accidents has made it off limits to us and is using the very man she wants to kill to stop people getting in. How thoroughly ironic.'

Amber cracked an eye open. '*Wait. Are you saying there are no humans in the event hall?*'

'Just the maintenance team,' I replied with a shrug.

Amber unfolded her body and arched her back. '*I think Devil Dog is right.*'

'*I am?*' asked Buster, sounding just as confused as I felt.

'*Though it pains me to admit it,*' my cat admitted. '*For once, which based on the law of averages had to happen, the dog came up with a good idea.*'

'*You're dang tooting, I did,*' Buster agreed. Then, after a pause, he ruined it all by asking. '*What was it?*'

Amber finished stretching and leapt down to the carpet.

'*Really, dog. Even when I cut you a break, you have to make it a chore. Felicity wants us to scope out the event hall.*'

'I do?' I questioned.

'*Yes,*' insisted my cat.

'Auntie, what's happening?' Mindy couldn't hear what I could, so was totally in the dark on what was being discussed.

She deserved an answer, but I was stuck in the middle of the conversation with my pets.

Amber was at the door, looking up at the handle as she always did when she wanted me to open it. Over her shoulder, she reminded me, '*You said that you cannot go in there but that you believe this Melissa woman is most likely destroying evidence, yes?*'

'That's right?' I agreed, frowning because Amber was never this forthcoming, never this voluntarily helpful.

'*So what is the obvious solution to your quandary?*' she posed the question in such a way that it was rhetorical, yet she was waiting for me to admit I needed to send the pets in.

I was being manipulated by my cat and I was not a fan.

'What are you up to?' I squinted at her, a pointless action since she wasn't looking my way.

Amber sighed. '*You want my help and moan that you don't get it. Then, when I offer it freely, you question my motive.*'

'Auntie, what is happening?' Mindy squealed in exasperation.

'Amber is offering to help,' I told her quickly, my concentration focused on Amber who was acting very out of character.

'That's good, right?' Mindy got off the bed. 'Amber and Buster can go into the event hall and snoop about without being spotted.'

'*The young one gets it,*' remarked my cat, still staring at the door handle.

Deeply suspicious, but more interested in finding out what might be going on in the event hall, I gave up arguing.

'Okay, you win,' I relented, throwing my hands in the air unable to believe I was allowing my cat to dictate our next move.

'*Super,*' murmured Amber, making it sound like there could never have been any other end result. '*Come along Devil Dog. It is time to go to work.*'

Honestly, looking back, I don't know how I managed to be so dumb.

We had to sneak around the back of the building to find a way in where we would not be seen. Reed's security team had the main entrance locked up tight, but a whole lot of visitors who expected to be inside already were milling around in the hotel lobby area. Getting through them would have been impossible anyway.

It meant a brisk trade for the hotel amenities - their coffee shop, boutique, and other services all getting more custom than usual. For us, it meant the bulk of the security guards were clustered there and no one was checking the Lipizzaner paddock at the very back of the hall.

Peering around the edge of the big doors where the horses were brought in and out by the team there with them, Mindy and I could hear people inside, but we could not see them. The electronic hum of what I took to be a podium either rising or lowering, told me the maintenance guys were doing as instructed to by Melissa. That, however, left a lot of hall space for her to be in.

Was she setting up her next attempt? Or was she clearing up the evidence of the most recent one? All I knew for sure was that she had kicked everyone out of the hall but chose to remain in there herself. Surely the deputy manager of such a big hotel had too many other important tasks that required her attention.

Well, not if I was right.

With a final hug for luck, I deployed my two secret spies. For once, they were not fighting. Amber was still acting strangely - cooperating and failing to fire snarky comments at the dog. She was never like this.

'Go to the door at the front when you are done,' I called after them. 'We'll collect you there.'

Amber's voice drifted back. *'We understand. This won't take long.'*

Both animals sidled around the edge of the door and vanished from sight.

Mindy caught me biting my top lip in worry.

'Don't worry, Auntie. They'll be fine. They can look after themselves.'

I wasn't so sure.

'Wah-Ha-Ha-ha-Haaaaaaa!' trumpeted a loud voice right behind us.

Both Mindy and I shrieked in fright, but where I came close to wetting myself and tried to run away, my niece's impulse reaction was to attack the unseen force at our rear.

The gap in time between the crazy noise behind me, and Mindy's spinning kick sending a high-heeled foot into the air was so short, I hadn't even had time to twitch my head around to see who was there.

The insane 'Wah-Ha-ha' turned instantly to a squeal of fright as Mindy's leg whipped through the air to almost remove Philippe's head.

'What the heck?' he squealed from the ground. To avoid the potential beheading, he'd had to fold his legs out and pray gravity did what it was supposed to do.

Mindy echoed his sentiment. 'Yes, Philippe! What the heck?'

I had a hand to my chest, holding it there until I felt my heart beating. One of the horses whinnied quietly behind me and I noted the abrupt absence of human conversation coming from inside the hall. A few seconds ago, we could hear the maintenance guys on the podium. Now I could not and that meant they must have heard our screams of fright.

'We need to go,' I whispered.

Mindy stepped over Philippe, offering a hand up, and pulling him onto his feet.

'You got me muddy,' the makeup artist complained, looking at his pink tartan trousers. He wore them over a pair of spats – a mode of footwear I had only ever seen adorning feet in old gangster movies. On top he had a satin shirt in a shade of pink that matched his trousers. It was edged with flamboyant ruffles on the cuffs and up the front where it buttoned. Over that was a purple leather jacket.

I couldn't guess where he shopped, but it wasn't anywhere I had ever looked for outfits.

We hurried away, the two young people bickering about not sneaking up on people and not trying to kill them when they did.

'What were you up to anyway?' asked Philippe. 'And what happened to the cat and the dog? Didn't I see you with some pets?'

Inside the event hall, Buster was trying to lead the way.

'*I should go first,*' he insisted. '*Superheroes always place themselves in harm's way to protect others.*'

Amber argued, '*Which would be fine if you were a real superhero and not a dribbling, fat dog. Do you even know where we are going?*' she enquired, jumping up onto a counter to get a better view of the hall's layout.

'*Back to Felicity's stand?*' he hazarded a guess.

That he was right came as a surprise to the cat but proved to aid her true purpose. '*That's right, Buster ...*'

'*Devil Dog,*' he corrected her.

'*You forgot to do the voice,*' she pointed out.

He dropped his voice an octave and made it sound like he'd been smoking cigars for forty years. '*Sorry. Devil Dog.*'

Amber puffed out a sigh, unhappy that her plan included the dog. '*Right, so we should split up and approach it from two directions.*'

'*Good thinking,*' rasped Buster.

'*You go straight on.*' Amber made sure Buster understood which way he was supposed to go. '*Keep out of sight and if you think you have been spotted, make sure you abort your route and double back to evade them. No attacking, understood?*'

Buster frowned up at the cat. '*Devil Dog does not attack innocent civilians. I am sworn to protect them.*'

131

Amber tried to take him seriously, but it was a real struggle not to roll her eyes.

*'Okay, Devil Dog. You go that way, and I will take the long route around. I'll meet you there. Remember, our task is to observe and report back to Felicity.'*

*'What if I spot her setting a new deadly device that will look like an accident when triggered? What if I can stop her and save lives by endangering my own?'*

Amber opened her mouth to tell Buster to stop being so ridiculously cavalier with his own safety but stopped herself. She wanted the house to herself and here was the perfect opportunity to achieve that. There was one spot on the couch that caught the sun almost the whole day. When she sat there, she could remain in one position for hours without having to move to track the sun's warming rays.

Buster always ruined it. The giant, slobbering idiot would climb up next to her and either flop down with such gusto that the resulting wave of dissipating energy would bounce her off the cushion, or he would quietly curl up next to her and deliberately seep gas from his back end right under her nose.

With a smile so cunning the dog couldn't hope to see it for what it was, Amber looked down at him.

*'Yes, good point, Devil Dog.'* Amber almost squeaked with excitement as she envisaged killing two birds with one stone. *'If there is a heroic and above all super macho way for you to die while saving the day, I say you should go for it. I will ensure they write songs about you.'*

Seeing no need for further discussion, Amber crossed the counter, leapt to a table, and vanished from sight.

132

'*Um, well, I didn't exactly mean that I should die,*' Buster called after her. '*More sort of make it look like I might so people get to witness my unbelievable bravery.*' No reply came back. '*Amber?*'

Buster looked in the direction she had gone for a few more seconds, questioning who might write songs about him if there was no one to see his incredible feats of heroism. Finding himself alone, he looked down to check his paws, questioning why they were not moving.

High above on a podium, two members of the hotel maintenance team were checking the structure.

'Did you see something?' asked Tony, the less work-inclined of the two.

Ralph, his colleague, was used to getting shackled with the lazy git and subsequently doing the brunt of the work. He'd missed breakfast though and was irritable.

'No, Tony, I did not see something because I am focused on doing what we were sent in here to do. Now, how about you help me so we can get this finished and I can get some brunch?'

'All right, all right, keep your hair on,' Tony continued to stare at the floor. 'It's not my fault your hangry.'

'Hangry?'

'Yes, hangry,' Tony explained. 'That's what they call it when a person gets grumpy because their belly is empty.'

Getting hangrier by the second, Ralph stopped checking bolts and fittings to poke his colleague in the ribs.

'Just what is it that you think you saw?' Ralph demanded to know. He doubted the lazy git had seen anything and was just using it as an excuse to avoid doing anything.

Tony missed his partners irritated tone. He was still squinting at the floor twenty feet below them.

'Looked like a cat and a dog having a conversation,' he remarked, not sure how else he could describe it.

Ralph punched him in his left kidney. Not hard enough to hurt, but with sufficient force to get Tony's attention.

Tony spun around, rocking the raised mobile platform. 'Whoa! What's that for?'

Ralph growled into his face. 'Help me check the structure and stop daydreaming.' Certain he was close to losing his temper and giving serious consideration to pushing Tony off the platform, Ralph busied himself with the structure again.

Tony stared at the floor for a few more seconds - long enough to show he wasn't jumping to it just because Ralph got upset, but not so long that he tested his colleague's patience.

Twenty feet below them and about fifty feet across, a bulldog had found his way into a dressmaker's stand.

He was dodging in and out of the various booths, creating his own secret route to get to his destination with the maximum amount of combat rolls thrown in.

One roll, when he chose to pretend there were six ninjas attacking him, landed him among a rack of dresses and samples of material and there an idea sprung to life.

134

It was going to take him a minute or maybe three to chew the material he found. He needed a hole he could get his head through for a start, but when he emerged from under the trailing dresses once more, peeking out to check for enemy forces, he was wearing a dark auburn cape.

He passed a mirror and paused, taking in his own reflection for a moment. The sheet of silk he found was twice as long as his body – all the better to flutter vividly when he ran, he told himself.

'*Goodness, I feel sexy,*' he murmured to himself as he preened and pranced, pawing the air, and making a noise that he hoped was like a tiger's mating call.

Remembering his mission, he set off again.

With Philippe in tow once more, we cut across the hotel's back courtyard where delivery vehicles would come in and out. Philippe had spotted us from the coffee shop in the lobby where he was avoiding his boss and lover (same person) and still refusing to work.

'It's not like he can fire me,' Philippe grinned. 'He's terrified his husband will find out about us.'

'No doubt,' I agreed, keeping my opinion on the subject to myself.

I didn't know how to answer his question about the pets but didn't have to because Mindy remarked on how well put together his outfit was. Philippe squealed with delight at the opportunity to talk about it and instantly forgot all about my cat and dog.

I had no idea how long Amber and Buster might need to complete their task. I was guessing Melissa was in there, but maybe she wasn't, and my pets would be at the event hall doors shortly. I would need to check periodically to see if they were waiting by the doors. The guards would no doubt question how the cat and dog got in there and I would bluff them with an easy lie about leaving them behind in all the earlier excitement.

Either way, I figured I had a few minutes before I needed to be back inside the hotel, so we crossed the road to visit a franchise coffee shop. Takeaway coffee cups were the perfect props. Any casual observers would think we had chosen to find a less-crowded coffee shop and hadn't been snooping around at the back of the event hall. Unfortunately, we were not alone in thinking the one in the hotel lobby was too crowded and found it to be filled with the overflow of bored couples here for the wedding fayre.

There could be no question that was who they were because it was the singular subject of conversation we could hear while waiting to be served. The general topic was to do with what the hold up might be and when they would open the doors.

Paying little attention as the queue crept forward, I hadn't noticed Mindy's hairdresser acquaintance Jessica ahead of us until she was handed her cup and turned to leave.

'Oh, hey,' she waved to Mindy and Philippe. I felt sure I was included in the same salutation somewhere rather than cut out because I am older.

The queue moved forward, and I was next in line. Jessica was on the other side of a small barrier intended to make queuing easier.

'Is your auntie okay?' Jessica enquired, keeping her voice low but not so low that I couldn't hear her. It was sweet that she was asking after me. 'I saw the accident. Wasn't it scary?'

Mindy puffed out a breath, making a relieved sound. 'For a moment there I thought she was a goner. I don't know where Vince came from, but he sure saved the day.'

The annoying voice in my head chose to agree while reminding me that I owed him big time. I hadn't given myself any time to process his big, concussed revelation yet. Ok, truthfully, every time I caught myself thinking about it, I found something else to do. I did not want to think about what I might want to say to him the next time we met.

Scarier yet was the idea that I owed him because I knew exactly how he would like to be repaid and that simply wasn't going to happen.

'Who is he?' asked Jessica. 'I thought I knew everyone at the fayre.'

'Oh, he's a private investigator,' Mindy revealed. 'He's got his own firm and everything. He's sweet for Auntie. That's why he was hanging about.'

'A private investigator?' questioned Jessica.

'Yeah, gurl,' squealed Philippe in his usual excited manner. 'Like Dick Tracy, but British.'

The queue moved forward again, and I missed the next part of what was being said because I was giving our order. When I was done and moved to the end of the counter to wait, Mindy and the others came with me, Jessica too as she seemed quite taken with the concept of there being a clandestine investigation going on.

Were we about to pick up another hanger-on? We really didn't need the pale-skinned redhead to tag along too. In fact, the bigger our group got, the more likely it was that Melissa would cotton on to us.

Nevertheless, the three youngsters had their heads together and were whispering like conspirators.

I leaned forward to tap Mindy on the arm. When she stood up straight, leaving the huddle to see what I wanted, I said, 'Shhhh. Secrets are best kept that way.'

'But it's Jessica,' my niece replied as if that were explanation enough.

'There are already enough of us to be called the *Famous Five*,' I flared my eyes.

Mindy frowned. 'Who are the *Famous Five*?'

Showing my age again, I tried to come up with a modern-day equivalent, failed and waved my hand to move the conversation along.

'I'm sure she is very sweet, but what if she sees Melissa doing something, approaches her, and gets killed because Melissa thinks Jessica is onto her.'

Mindy gasped and nodded. 'Good point, Auntie. We haven't told her about Melissa yet.'

'What about Melissa?' asked Jessica.

I slapped a hand to my forehead.

As understanding dawned, Jessica's mouth dropped open. 'Oh, my goodness, she's behind it? Why?'

I clamped a hand over Philippe's mouth when he opened it to explain.

'You are best off not knowing,' I assured her. 'We are just exploring a possibility that Melissa might be involved, that's all. We have no evidence of any wrongdoing, just a theory we need to explore.'

Then Jessica asked something that sent a jolt through me.

'Is it to do with her husband?'

Amber sauntered along a steel beam high above the stands filling the event hall. Had she been able to, she might have whistled a happy tune. The humans were all gone which meant she could proceed without concern for who might see her, and the dog was off doing goodness knows what on a daft mission for Felicity.

If she got really lucky, the dog was going to get himself killed when he inadvertently triggered the next booby trap.

It didn't bother Amber that she had lied to Felicity. The human woman was just the person who inhabited her house and brought her food. Amber quite liked her, but Felicity could be replaced in a heartbeat, and it wasn't in a cat's nature to feel remorse or pity or any other weak emotion.

She was a hunter, ultimately, and there was no ignoring the drive inside her to take down one of the giant white birds.

They were below her now as she looked down, waddling here and there, or sitting with their feet tucked under their bodies. The cage of doves was at one end of the swan enclosure – another tempting target to consider.

The swans were big. Too big possibly, but that was no reason not to give it another go. They caught her by surprise last time, almost crushing her as they panicked and fought to repel the invading predator. This time, she was going to pick just one target, one who was asleep and would not see her attack until it was too late.

Then she would pounce and … she chuckled, '*The cat really will be among the pigeons.*'

Fifty yards away, in the cake stand across from Felicity's booth, Devil Dog was disappointed to find no more than a few crumbs to snuffle up. The firm displaying their goods had not yet been able to set their freshly baked cakes out.

Giving up on his quest for a snack, Buster turned his attention to Felicity's booth. There was no one there. The lighting gantry, which Buster would not have been able to identify anyway, was gone, removed by other members of the maintenance team once they established it was beyond repair and could not be remounted.

The event organiser told them to throw it on the scrap pile so that was what they did. She said there was more than enough light, and no one would notice the one slightly darker spot – each stand caused shadows anyway.

Buster sniffed around. There was no one here and if he understood his mission correctly, there ought to be a woman doing something sneaky somewhere in the event hall. The only humans he'd seen thus far were the two high up in the air on the moving platform thingy.

Was that something to do with it?

Unsure what his next move should be – he was a dog of action, not one who planned – he settled in to wait for Amber.

Two minutes later, getting bored from the inaction and thinking that he really needed to find another mirror in which he could check his magnificent profile, he set off.

His nose told him Amber was nowhere nearby and that meant the devious moggy had probably tricked him. She would be doing something catty, and he was going to let her get on with it.

Maybe this time Felicity would see what an utter, utter cat she was and return her to the rehoming centre she got her from. Buoyed by that thought, Buster chose to investigate the only humans he'd seen so far – the ones on the mobile platform.

Felicity believed there were humans doing wrong in here and he was the dog to put a stop to it.

## The Truth

The hotel lobby area was still littered with huffing future brides and bored future grooms all checking their watches and moaning about the delay.

We discovered the coffee shop was doling out free beverages to compensate for the wait and to keep people where they were. I could have saved myself a few quid, but I didn't need the money that badly and if I thought the queue across the road was bad, the one in here was three times the length.

Jessica was still asking questions, but I was trying to wheedle out of her why she thought this might be to do with Melissa's husband, Reed. What had she seen or heard that made her think that?

Begging a moment's grace when Jessica asked me what she could do to help, I touched Mindy's arm to get her attention.

'Can you check to see if Amber and Buster are at the door? If there is nothing for them to see, they could already be waiting.'

Mindy nodded, weaving through the press of people around the event hall doors. Philippe went with her, leaving me with Jessica.

This was better. It would give me a chance to pick her brains without the overly excitable Philippe jumping in when a random thought made his jaw work.

I shuffled around to face her again, only to find that she was gone.

Blinking in my confusion, I looked around but could see no sign of her. I guessed she had finished her coffee and shot off to find a restroom quickly. When someone caught gently hold of my elbow, I figured it was her returning.

However, when I spun around to see, it wasn't her face in front of me, it was Reed's chest. I looked up to find his face.

'Mrs Philips, I've been trying to find you. How are you doing?' There was concern etched on his features. He was referring to the fact that I'd suffered two near misses in under twenty-four hours, each of which could have killed me.

As I went to answer, I spotted Melissa looking my way. It was only a glance as she made her way across the lobby to the event hall doors and the security team stationed there. She was probably looking at Reed, her target, and not me at all, but I had to wonder what murderous thought might be going through her mind.

In that moment, I made a decision and grabbed Reed's hand.

'Is there somewhere private we can go?' I made my words urgent and demanding. 'I need to ask you about something?'

Reed's brow wrinkled, unsure what my something might be, but after a second, he nodded and twitched his head back toward the busy hotel reception area.

'We can talk back here. I have an office right behind reception.'

I swung my head around to look for Mindy, spotting Philippe first because ... well, because he stands out. It's a bit like having a room full of people and then Bugs Bunny walks in. You cannot help but notice him. They were only just getting to the doors and would be able to see if my pets were there or not. I watched to see if they would turn around so I could wave my intention to go with Reed, but they didn't, and I gave up.

They wouldn't wander far when they couldn't find me. Unlike Jessica who still hadn't returned. I wanted to find out what she knew but warning Reed took priority now.

The din of background conversation dropped sharply when Reed led me through the door behind reception and then fell to nothing when he closed the door to his private office.

Reed indicated a chair for me to sit in.

'I would offer you a drink, Mrs Philips but …' He placed the plastic sports water bottle he always seemed to carry on his desk and turned to face me.

I wiggled the coffee cup in my hand, acknowledging that there was no need for him to act as my host, and got straight down to business.

'Reed do you think the two incidents were accidents?' I asked, edging around the topic, and easing him into it rather than just spring it on him.

I got a single quizzical raised eyebrow in response. 'What else would they be, Mrs Philips? We already explored the idea that Mrs Green might be behind the first one, and I must repeat that I don't think she was. Not for one minute.'

'No,' I allowed myself a lopsided smile. 'I was off the mark with that one, I'll admit. No, Primrose Green is not behind what happened. Not that I would put it beyond her to attempt to sabotage my stand,' I added quickly. 'However …' I found myself struggling to work out how to broach the subject at hand.'

'What is it, Mrs Philips?' Reed encouraged. 'If you have a safety concern, please tell me what it is.'

Still struggling, I decided to go for broke.

'I think someone is trying to kill you but in such a way that it looks like an accident.'

Reed's eyes locked on mine for a moment, the air and everything else in the room completely silent and still.

'Why, Mrs Philips? Why would someone be trying to kill me?' He held up a hand to stop me answering as he added a third question. 'Better yet, who do you think it is?'

Now I was stuck. Did I tell him? If I revealed my suspicions and gave him Melissa's name, would he play it cool and help me to catch her out? Or would he storm from the room and confront her? There was only one way to find out.

'It's Melissa,' I stated boldly, making myself sound as confident as possible.

Again, Reed just stared at me. It lasted for a few seconds, giving me the impression he expected me to say something else.

'Melissa, Melissa?' he questioned. 'My Melissa. Melissa that I am currently married to.'

'Yes. Melissa Cartwright, your wife. The deputy manager of this hotel and the wedding fayre event organiser. That Melissa.' I felt we had covered sufficiently now who it was we were discussing.

Reed settled back onto the edge of his desk, frowning deeply as he studied my face.

'What would lead you to draw that conclusion, Mrs Philips?'

I hit him with cold eyes.

'Because she knows about your affair. That young woman I saw you with last night. Do you deny being involved with her?'

'Kimberly?' he questioned. 'No. No, I don't deny it. I intend to marry her just as soon as the divorce is finalised.' He saw the surprise register on my face and ploughed on. 'I left Melissa as soon as I acknowledged my feelings for Kimberly.' He wasn't looking at my eyes anymore, not that he was trying to avoid the judgement in my gaze. Rather, he was staring into nowhere, his thoughts focused on the very real possibility that his wife might be trying to kill him. 'She is upset about the divorce,' he admitted.

'She was right beside my booth yesterday when the first 'accident' happened, Reed. Why were you there?'

He snapped his head up, his eyes going wide in shock. 'Melissa called me to go there.'

I tipped my head to the side and gave him a sorry smile – I was right, whether he wanted to believe it or not.

'Oh, my goodness. I got a call on the radio about a minute before it all happened. Could I meet her at the event hall entrance? Your stand is the first one people come to when they enter the event hall.'

'I know,' I pointed out, holding back from adding that I selected it on purpose because I am smart.

The colour had drained from Reed's face, and he was mumbling in his disbelief. 'She called me there knowing I would be right next to the electrified stand.'

'Yes,' I nodded. 'She needed it to look like an accident, so she cut the wire, and just before you got there, she connected it to the steel structure of my booth. Someone was going to touch the steel and get fried,' I cringed at my own choice of words. 'I believe she knew you would rush to their aid and most likely get yourself killed in the process.'

'But she could have killed everyone in the booth,' Reed pointed out, not presenting an argument but reeling from the magnitude of it.

All I could do was agree. 'It would still look like an accident.'

'Oh, my goodness,' he whispered.

I continued to hammer home my proof. 'This morning, when the lighting gantry fell, who could have accessed it? Who was close by when it fell?'

Reed looked like he needed to lie down but levered himself off his desk to cross the room. I wondered where he was going until he pulled a half empty – or half full depending on one's life philosophy – bottle of Scottish whisky from behind a file.

He offered it first to me, and when I shook my head, he popped off the lid and took a healthy belt of the dark liquid.

'For my nerves,' he explained. 'I need to get another look at that gantry. She was standing ten feet away when that fell. I remember heading over to speak with Mrs Green and that was when it fell. It missed me by the width of a hair.'

'If you hadn't moved when you did, it would have killed you,' I agreed.

'And you,' he reminded me. 'She was prepared to harm others to get to me. All because I want a divorce?'

I gave him a shrug. 'Never underestimate a scorned woman's wrath. You left her, pushing her from your life so you could be happy with a younger, prettier woman.'

'But we were never great together,' Reed protested. 'We fought half the time, and we were too young when we got married.'

'Is that how she felt?' I challenged him.

Reed fell silent, his lack of response enough to give me my answer. The silence didn't last long though. After two seconds, he screwed the lid back on his bottle, slammed it down on his desk and straightened his jacket.

'I have to confront her. I'm going to put an end to this before she can hurt anyone else.'

He made a beeline for his office door, forcing me to step into his path to stop him from leaving.

'You can't.'

'The heck I can't!' he raised his voice.

'You have no evidence. If I am right, then Melissa is guilty of murder, or manslaughter maybe. The point is, Douglas Irwin died yesterday because of her actions and Vince Slater could have died a few hours ago when that lighting gantry came down. When she laughs in your face, what will you do?'

Seeing my point, he asked, 'What do you propose?'

## Gremlins?

Once again, Buster took a meandering route on his way to the podium. He ran across open spaces, minimising his exposed time, and kept to the shadows as much as possible. Where he could, he clambered under counters to peer out at floor level before moving on and threw in combat roll after combat roll. Until he began to feel queasy, that is, at which point he decided walking might be better for the last twenty yards.

Ten yards beyond Tony and Ralph working high above the event hall floor, Amber was sitting on top of the outer wall of a vintage wedding car hire firm's stand. The value of the Rolls Royce beneath her fluffy derriere was of no interest to her. She'd been watching the swans for the last ten minutes, biding her time, and carefully selecting her target.

It was a single move, just one leap to get to the swan she planned to attack. It was asleep, its head wrapped around its back, and wouldn't know she was coming. None of them would, until she landed on its head. Then it was nothing more than a case of hanging on as the rest of the swans scattered.

This would be bragging rights. Provided Felicity let her take it home once she'd dragged its carcass back to their room.

That was going to take some effort, she acknowledged, but nothing was going to put her off now. She was yet to hear the dog exploding or getting fried so maybe she could employ him as brute strength to drag the dead swan.

With that thought in her head, she twitched her tail, bunched all her muscles, and leapt.

Tony and Ralph were descending back to floor level. They hadn't found a single loose bolt, damaged cable, or anything else that would suggest the structure was in any way unsafe.

That message had already been relayed to Mrs Cartwright the event organiser. She was outside waiting to hear that the podium was parked outside again and that the firms displaying their wares and services were safe to come back in. The stallholders would get half an hour before the impatient visitors were finally allowed in.

Ralph didn't care about any of that. Every day was just another day for him. He came to work, fixed a bunch of broken-down stuff, and went home again. Some days were better than others. Some days he found himself shackled with Tony who had spent the last ten minutes suggesting they didn't need to check the last few square yards because everything else they'd checked so far had been fine.

Mostly, Ralph wanted to get off the podium and away from his colleague. Otherwise, he was going to hit him on the head with a handy wrench. He'd even selected which one he wanted to use.

Movement caught Ralph's eye.

Tony saw his partner twitch and focus on a single point.

'Was it the cat again?' he asked with a trace of sarcasm. 'Or the dog?'

Ralph shook his head, uncertain of what he had seen.

'That was not a cat. It was five times too big and …'

'And …' Tony prompted.

'It was wearing a cape,' Ralph concluded, knowing what he had seen but uncertain he should believe his eyes had it right.

Buster had grown bored of sneaking around. Felicity wanted him to find the person behind the supposed accidents and sent him here. After that, he got a little woolly about what he was expected to do, but Felicity said a piece of the structure fell down and hurt Vince, nearly killing her in the process.

Now the only humans in the event hall were the two he could see in the air, and they had been up there fiddling with the structure.

Maybe they were good guys, maybe they were not, but in the same way that he treated the postman, or anyone else who ever came to the door, as a probable attacker to be repelled, he was going to act first and ask questions later.

Drawing in a deep lungful of air, he planted his paws, came into the open where he saw the humans looking down at him and roared his death cry.

'Dun dun, Dah!'

'Is that dog attacking us?' asked Tony.

Ralph made no attempt to answer, he had a different question. 'Why is it wearing a cape?'

Their podium was almost all the way down now, and Ralph's hand was hovering on the control, questioning whether he should go back up a few feet. Just far enough that the crazy barking dog couldn't get to them while he radioed for help.

The explosion of hissing, squawking, and bugling of alarm from the swans made both men spin through one hundred and eighty degrees.

'What the heck was that?' gasped Tony, watching a spray of feathers shoot into the air. It looked like someone had just fired a shotgun into a pillow.

Ralph didn't answer, he was too busy tracking the sounds.

They were coming his way.

Amber stuck her landing perfectly. The swan, a large male, awoke with a startled bellow which shocked all the other swans.

They all went in one direction – away from the swan now wearing a cat necktie. However, their direction of travel combined with speed, panic, and the uniformity in which they then hit the dove cage, sent it toppling.

In turn, the dove cage had enough weight to rip through the side wall of the swans' enclosure. It hit the floor and burst open, sending the small white birds into the air. With the side of their enclosure missing, and since they were all already running in that direction, the swans just kept on going.

When Amber retold the story to the neighbour's cat, Celeste, she would leave out the part where she got thrown clear and chipped one of her back teeth. It happened when the swan she clung to flapped its wings and attempted to take off.

Spinning out of control, Amber did not land on her feet, but rather on her face. As the panicked swans charged into the stands of the wedding fayre, and the doves took to the air, Amber sat back onto her haunches, licked a paw, and nonchalantly began to clean and straighten her fur.

Buster was running at maximum velocity when he heard the eruption of swans. He pricked his ears up, scanning ahead for what might be making the noise but was moving too fast to alter course when a dozen insane white birds burst into sight and came straight for him.

The shocking sight made him bark, and faced with a new threat, the swans wheeled right.

Outside the entrance to the event hall, the security guards were all turning to face inward. The glass door provided a view into the hall, but there wasn't anything to see. The mobile podium had descended as expected – the chaps had already declared the job of inspecting the structure complete, but now there was noise echoing around the hall and it sounded like bedlam.

Tony and Ralph were already taking the podium upward again to avoid the cape-wearing dog, when they saw swans coming. The doves, free and looking to escape shot upward as a small white flock, and finding ceiling where they felt there ought to be sky, they circled.

Tony and Ralph hunkered down inside the platform's protective cage.

Melissa's voice burst over their radio. 'What's going on in there?'

She'd been waiting outside for the all-clear but wasn't waiting any longer. She shoved the doors open and strode in with half a dozen of Reed's guards on her heels.

In his office Reed got her radio message.

'Reed can you get to the event hall? There is something happening here!'

He met Felicity's eyes, the two exchanging a look.

'Do you think this is a trap?' he asked, basically questioning if he was being lured to his death.

Felicity closed her eyes for a second and groaned inwardly. She knew Amber and Buster were in the event hall. If there was an incident developing, it was bound to have her pets behind it.

Rather than admit that, she said, 'Too public. Everyone heard that message, right?'

'Everyone with a radio. I must go, Mrs Philips. I will be wary of my wife and will catch up with you shortly so we can come up with a plan.'

A plan was needed, but as Felicity followed the head of security from the room, she was buoyed with a sense that they might now catch the guilty person. With the killer's intended victim now in the know and on her side, she felt her chances of success were greatly improved.

The swans were looking for a way out. By the time Melissa burst through the doors at the other end of the event hall, three of them were airborne and heading for the light they could see. It was coming through panels in the large roller door at the back.

Right where the horses were.

The Lipizzaners might be the best trained and most placid horses in the world but low-flying, giant white birds trumpeting their terror was too much even for them to ignore.

The flying swans only spotted the lack of actual escape route at the last moment and had to bank hard to avoid hitting the roller door. It meant a second pass over the heads of the panicked horses.

High above the event hall floor, Tony and Ralph watched the caped Bulldog perform a power slide in which he wiped out a six-foot-high display of flowers and reversed direction. The swans, those that were still on the ground, were running back toward him.

They in turn were attempting to get away from the thundering hooves of the Lipizzaner horses who were running from the flying swans who were not, in fact, even behind them anymore.

Watching it all with mild amusement from a vantage spot across the hall, Amber licked her paw and used it to wash behind her left ear.

Reed arrived at the entry doors, bursting through them to join his soon-to-be ex-wife as they and the other security guards all gawped at the madness unfolding in the event hall.

The exact nature of the drama could not be seen — it was obscured by the stands and booths of the various traders, however they could all hear it, most especially the sound of things crashing and breaking.

Melissa managed to get her brain up to speed, instructing Reed to get everyone. When asked to clarify what that might mean, she demanded he rustle up all his security, all the guys from maintenance, and all the stall holders. If they were going to salvage anything from this event, they would need all hands on deck.

Felicity, who had poked her head through the doors of the event hall to confirm her worst thoughts were accurate, ducked back out, flared her eyes meaningfully at Mindy, and twitched her head in the direction of the hotel's main entrance.

They were going to try to find Amber and Buster before anyone else did.

Buster, meanwhile, was arguing with himself about what he ought to be doing. He was running away, and that was not an approved Devil Dog activity. Devil Dog should run toward danger.

The cape looked good though.

'What the heck was that?' asked Melissa. Something that looked suspiciously like a baked potato with feet just shot through an intersection fifty yards away. It was only visible for a half second but whatever it was appeared to be wearing a cape.

'Do you think maybe it was a gremlin?' asked a maintenance man called Arthur. 'Gremlins would explain the current spate of problems. Gremlins will chew through cables and loosen bolts.'

Melissa offered the man a withering look. It was enough to silence his pointless wittering. She had no idea what she might have just seen and mostly hoped she never saw it again.

'Get the animals rounded up and back into their pens,' she ordered the men assembled around her. 'Find Mr Flintlock, he owns the swans, and keep the visitors out.' Delivered in a tone that brooked no argument, Melissa watched as the hotel staff fanned out.

Someone was messing with her well-oiled machine. This was the fifth time she had helmed the wedding fayre, the biggest event the hotel ran each year, and there had never been so much as a cut finger before.

Just looking at the event hall from her position by the doors, she could tell they were not going to open to the public today.

There were going to be questions asked by her superiors after the event ended. They were already calling for a report on the death yesterday. They hadn't yet heard about the second incident this morning and would likely go nuts when they did.

Were there more casualties now?'

Grimacing with anger, Melissa promised herself she was going to find out who was behind this latest debacle and see they were arrested.

The guilty person – at least, the one guilty of the untold destruction inside the event hall, was making her way back to the door she originally came in through. Felicity's instructions were to go to the doors at the other end, but there were humans there now and they sounded quite agitated.

Amber hadn't caught herself a swan, but she had taken down a pair of doves and all in all felt pretty good about her day.

As she trotted contentedly along the upper steelwork of a dressmaker's stall, she spotted the stupid dog going by beneath her.

'*Hey, Buster,*' she called out to get his attention.

Buster was no longer being pursued by angry swans, horses, or anything else, but like Amber, had seen the swarming horde of humans as something to avoid so had been heading back to where he came in.

Spotting Amber high above him, he corrected her, '*Devil Dog.*'

'*Yeah, I'm not calling you that.*'

'*You were earlier.*'

'*That's when I wanted to trick you into doing things. You are always so unsuspecting, Buster. So … dumb. What's with the cape?*'

'*Isn't it cool!*' Buster barked, proud about his wardrobe addition.

'Buster!'

Both cat and dog put their ears up at the sound of Felicity's voice. Buster's bark was loud enough for her to hear, and her shout gave them a point to go to.

The shouting humans were coming closer as they filled the aisles and passages between the stalls. Now was the time to be somewhere else.

'There's that gremlin again!' shouted Arthur, spotting Buster once more.

The dog took off, hurtling around a corner and out of sight once more.

'That wasn't a gremlin,' argued, Dennis, another long-serving member of the maintenance team. 'It looked more like a fat badger to me.'

Arthur frowned deeply. 'How many badgers wear capes to your knowledge?' he challenged.

I was relieved to see my pets approaching, both Amber and Buster appeared at the same time and were moving fast. Amber jumped down from the roof of a supercar rental stand onto the bonnet of a Ferrari and then to the floor. Buster, running as fast as his stumpy legs would carry him, kept going until he was almost too close to stop, then folded out his legs to perform a belly slide the final few yards.

'*Dun dun, Dah!*'

'Where did he get a cape?' Mindy wanted to know.

I had no idea, but I was too focused on my cat to pay Buster any attention.

'You never had any intention of helping, did you, Amber?' I scolded her.

We had retrieved both animals and were hurrying back to the street once more. That my pets were to blame for the bedlam inside was not in question. Not so far as I was concerned.

'*I don't know what you are talking about,*' protested Amber, settling into my arms as we hurried along the pavement to get back to the hotel.

I lifted her into the air as I walked, holding her so we were face to face.

'Amber you have white feathers sticking out of your mouth.'

'*I found a shuttlecock to play with,*' she lied.

'You tricked me, Amber. I knew you were being too nice to Buster.'

'*Devil Dog,*' he corrected me as he led the way along the street. '*Look, I even have a cape. Now all I need is a mask to hide my true identity and maybe a utility collar I can store ninja throwing stars and things like that in.'*

Amber shrugged at me. *'I'm a cat. We are devious. Really you should be pointing the finger of blame at yourself for trying to change my nature. Anyway, there wasn't anyone doing anything in there. I got up high to look about and the only humans in the event hall were two men on a platform checking the structure. Melissa was nowhere in sight.'*

'Auntie, what's she saying?' asked Mindy.

Philippe shot her a look, twitching his eyes from her to me and to Amber and then back to Mindy. 'Saying?' he questioned.

Without shifting her gaze, Mindy told him, 'Auntie can hear what the animals are saying.'

His right eyebrow hiked to the top of his head where it merged with his hairline.

'Trust me on this,' Mindy assured him. 'Why do you think she sent them into the hall? They were gathering information on what was going on because they can move about without being seen.

'I sure hope they weren't seen,' I remarked. Plenty of people knew I had a cat and a dog with me. If the trail of destruction inside the event hall were traced back to them, I would have a lot of explaining to do. Worse yet, I knew almost all the people selling their services and goods this weekend and it is a small community. Upsetting them all would do me no favours.

Philippe wasn't sure what to make of Mindy's claim or the fact that I hadn't denied it. We were back at the hotel entrance though, and now had to run the gauntlet of people inside while praying no one put two and two together.

I held my breath as we crossed the lobby, my heart banging in my chest by the time we got to the elevator.

'Do you think they will open again today?' Mindy wanted to know.

I managed a weary chuckle. 'No. I didn't get a good look, but when I came through the hall doors behind Reed, I could see swans in the air and horses charging through the aisles. I reckon today is a total write off.'

The elevator pinged and the doors swished open on our floor.

'What does this mean for our investigation then?' asked Mindy as she stepped out. 'What do we do about Melissa? Do you think she will strike again, or will she be too distracted now that she has all that mess to deal with? Should we warn Reed, do you think?'

Of course, I hadn't told them about my conversation with the hotel's head of security yet.

'There has been a development,' I announced. 'Reed is in the picture.'

'You told him?' questioned Mindy. 'How did he react to that?'

'Wait,' implored Philippe, getting left behind. 'How did who react to what? Who is Reed?'

'The head of security,' Mindy filled the makeup artist in quickly. 'He's the one Melissa is trying to kill because he is having an affair.'

'Actually, they split up,' I updated her. 'But he admits Melissa is unhappy about the impending divorce.'

'Naturally,' agreed Mindy. 'So is he going to help us catch her?'

163

'I think so.' I held Amber up in front of my face. 'We were about to discuss how we might lure Melissa into tipping her hand when this one,' I glared at the cat, 'caused pandemonium in the event hall. I will catch up with him again shortly.'

'Can I talk to the dog?' asked Philippe. He'd been totally focused on both my pets since Mindy revealed the truth about my unique ability. 'Or the cat,' he added. 'This is such a weird concept and I want to test it out.'

Mindy cocked her head to one side.

'You mean it's too outlandish to believe and you need to prove to yourself that what I told you is true.'

Philippe's cheeks coloured, though it wasn't easy to see under the rouge he wore.

His request interrupted what we were talking about – Melissa wasn't behind the 'accidents' and we were back to square one. I let it go though, curious to see how the makeup artist might react when he accepted the truth.

'Go ahead,' I encouraged, as I opened the door to my room and went in. 'Ask them to do something and see what happens.'

Philippe was a sceptic, we discovered. With a finger raised to make a point, he said, 'But they must understand a certain amount of human speech, so if I ask them to do something and they do it, it could be nothing more than coincidence.'

Frowning, Mindy said, 'Okay. What do you propose?'

'I will whisper something to the dog, and he will then pass it on to you,' he indicated to make it clear he meant me and not Mindy. 'No one else will have heard it so if you repeat back what I said, I guess I will have to accept that.'

Hardly a challenge at all.

'Please,' I invited him to do his worst.

Philippe knelt at Buster's side, cupping his hands around the dog's left ear so he could cover his lips for extra secrecy.

Buster whipped his head around to glare at the young makeup artist and gave his response.

I burst out laughing.

Mindy's forehead crinkled in question. 'What did he say, Auntie?'

I was laughing so much I was choking and had to take a bottle of mineral water from the minibar to get it under control.

Philippe was sitting on the end of my bed, his own face frowning with confusion.

'So come on, what did he say?' Philippe wanted to know.

'I assume you insulted him?' I guessed.

Philippe's jaw dropped open.

'*He said I have a face like a heap of discarded towels,*' complained Buster.

I relayed that to Philippe who looked about ready to faint.

Knowing Buster, Mindy was smiling when she asked, 'What did Buster say?' she too was keen to hear what had made me laugh so hard.

'His reply to Philippe was that he has a face like a baboon's scrotum.' I assumed my dog was referring to the colourful undercarriage some species of monkey or baboon have. In truth, I don't know a monkey from an ape, but the mental image was all that mattered.

Mindy giggled, covering her face to hide it because Philippe clearly wasn't happy with the comparison.

The phone next to my bed rang, pausing my involvement in the conversation as I crossed the room to answer it.

Mindy and Philippe continued talking, the makeup artist willing to believe I could understand my animals but struggling still to wrap his head around the idea.

'Felicity Philips,' I answered the hotel phone, curious to discover who might be calling me on it.

'Mrs Philips, this is Reed Cartwright, head of hotel security.' He was being very formal. I was about to question why when I realised he must have Melissa standing close by and felt a need to hide what he knew.

Playing it cool in case I could be overheard, I said, 'How can I help you?'

There was a moment's pause before he said, 'There has been some damage to your booth, Mrs Philips. All the other stallholders are in the event hall inspecting their stands and attempting to put everything back together. I thought you came into the hall behind me.'

'I did,' I admitted, 'But … well, there seemed to be a lot going on.'

'Yes,' Reed concurred. 'Are you able to come down to the event hall, Mrs Philips?'

166

'Of course. I will be there momentarily.'

'Do they know it was Amber and Buster?' asked Mindy when I put the phone down.

'*It was all her doing*,' insisted Buster, making sure the finger of blame pointed firmly at the cat.

Amber had one back leg stretched out as she hunched over it. Preening again, she had the air of a creature who cared not one bit for the concerns of others. I wondered if it ought to concern me that cats are basically cute, furry sociopaths.

Picking up my handbag – my usual one, not the stupidly expensive Flirkin one – I checked I had everything and started toward the door.

'He didn't say. I think he was being cautious with his words because Melissa was within earshot. We'll find out soon enough.' I gave her my reply while my hand rested on the door handle ready to open it.

'*Are we going out again?*' asked Buster, still wearing his cape and wagging his tail.

His tail stopped when I said, 'Just the humans this time.'

In the quiet of the elevator car as it descended to the ground floor, I put some more thought into what we needed to do. To catch Melissa, we needed to see her doing something that would result in a dangerous accident but somehow also prevent anyone from getting hurt. Would we find something damning when we inspected the lighting gantry or was Melissa so far ahead of us that she had already made sure any evidence had been removed?

We were on the back foot for sure and this was a cagey game fraught with danger because we had to let her do something before we could catch her.

Just how we might achieve that, I had no idea, but prayed with Reed's help, we might be able to come up with something. Perhaps he could assign a couple of his guards to carefully follow her around.

I was still deep in thought when Mindy tapped my arm. The elevator doors were open, and people were waiting to get in.

I mumbled an apology and followed my niece. She and Philippe led the way to the event hall but getting there was not the plain sailing I hoped it might be.

Crossing the lobby, a man's voice shouted out, 'Oi!'

Philippe swore.

'Hey, Philippe,' the man called again. It was impossible to miss the anger in his voice, and had there been any question, his stomping advance would have removed it.

He was over six feet tall and the same width at his shoulders and belly. Well into his fifties, his lustrous brown hair was far from the original colour, which was most likely grey if he ever stopped dying it. Unlike Philippe he wore no make up but was sporting a dangly gold chandelier like earring from his left earlobe.

'I don't want to talk to you, Henri,' Philippe raised a dismissive hand, palm out and shied his face away from the man.

I guessed correctly that this was his employer and married lover.

Mindy reached for the small of her back, the movement subtle and unnoticed by the advancing man. I knew to expect it and used my own hand to pin Mindy's in place before she could slide out whatever weapon she had secured there.

'You are being unreasonable, Philippe,' Henri complained, his tone and ire diminishing. 'You knew I was married at the start.'

Philippe was not listening to reason. 'It's over Henri. This ship has sailed. Philippe does not get two-timed.'

Henri's face darkened, his anger returning. 'Oh, yeah? Well, you still work for me, Philippe. They are opening the wedding fayre in the next half hour, and I expect you back at your table impressing anyone who comes into my booth.'

'Or what?' demanded Philippe, throwing down the gauntlet.

'Or you're fired,' snarled Henri.

It was enough of a threat to make Philippe gasp. 'You wouldn't!'

Henri had a triumphant sneer on his face when he said, 'Try me.'

Mindy twisted her head to look at me, a question on her lips.

'He works for me,' I blurted. He didn't, of course, and I had never employed a makeup artist at any point in my career. I outsourced all such work, recommending firms I knew by reputation while charging a fee for pushing work their way. Quite what I was going to do with a makeup artist I had no idea.

'What's going on, Henri?' asked another man, one of four coming up behind Philippe's boss. The one who spoke was dressed dandily much like Philippe, but the other three – an all-male makeup artist team, looked straight.

With his sneer still in place, Henri nodded his head at me. 'This one thinks she can poach Philippe.'

'I am not your property, Henri,' snapped Philippe. 'I will work for whom I want.' Message delivered, he twisted his torso around to look at me with worried eyes. He dropped his voice to a whisper. 'Seriously, this could be trouble. Did you mean what you said about giving me a job?'

I had no idea what I was going to do with him, but it was too late to take it back now. I nodded.

The five makeup artists formed up like a wall, their threat unspoken but visibly there.

Mindy tensed the arm behind her back, shooting her eyes at me to ask permission to engage. For Mindy, a nineteen-year-old woman with a few anger issues and a thirst for evening out the scales of justice where gender equality came into play, this was probably a great opportunity.

I felt that we had already generated enough havoc this weekend.

'Is there a problem here?'

We all turned to find Melissa giving Henri and his friends a smile that was engaging but had don't-push-your-luck written all over it. She was able to read the situation and aim her carefully worded warning at the right people, but it still unnerved me to have the killer coming to my rescue.

Flanking her on either side were two members of hotel security. They were big men with unreadable expressions. It was enough to convince Henri this was not the time and place for a heated discussion.

Henri looked Melissa up and down disdainfully and dismissed her.

'You're fired,' he spat at Philippe with a laugh. 'Don't think this is over though.' He was starting to back up but hadn't finished issuing threats yet. 'No one leaves me short-handed.'

I let go a sigh of relief when he finally turned around and walked away. This weekend had been far, far more stressful than I ever expected.

No one said anything until Henri and his friends had gone back into the event hall. An uncharitable voice in my head hoped his booth was one of those wrecked by the horses.

Melissa's voice got my attention. 'Um, Mrs Philips, there have been reports of a cat seen in the vicinity of Feathered Guests,' she named the firm who brought the swans and doves. 'You wouldn't happen to know anything about that, would you?'

I had half expected this and had been telling myself I would just come clean. However, she posed the question in such an uncertain manner, I had to question if she believed it herself.

'What sort of cat was it?' I asked. Lots of people knew I had Amber with me.

Melissa frowned a little. 'It was described as a large, domesticated cat with cream fur and a grey face.'

'Oh,' I faked surprise. 'Mine is a grey tabby,' I lied through my teeth. I felt bad but would pray extra hard for forgiveness next Sunday in church.

Whether she believed me or not, she chose to accept my answer and move on to the next topic.

'Despite how it looks in there, most of the damage is cosmetic or superficial.' I breathed a sigh of relief. 'We are going to open the doors as soon as we can, so I need to get all the vendors back in. Together we can assess the damage, create a priority list, and focus resources to the stands that require the most help.'

'So you want us to check out how bad ours is and let you know?'

Melissa nodded, setting off to go back into the event hall.

'Yours isn't too bad, but your brochure display got trampled.'

It was a trivial problem and I honestly felt terrible that in pursuit of a killer I had damaged the property of my fellows in the wedding industry. If I got the chance to make amends one day, I would.

'Did Mrs Green's booth suffer any damage?' I asked as casually as I could. Secretly I hoped it looked like the epicentre of the Hiroshima bomb, but kept that to myself.

Melissa held the door open for me to go into the hall. 'No, Mrs Philips. Remarkably, Mrs Green's stand survived unscathed.

I pulled a face and said unkind words in my head.

Mindy tapped Philippe on the arm. 'Come on, newest member of the team, let's get this place straightened out.'

172

I let them get to it, scouting about to spot Reed. Now that Melissa had left me, heading off to deal with other tasks, I could get back to conspiring to catch her.

I wanted to go searching for Reed, but Melissa had stopped just a couple of stalls up from us and her presence continued to make me nervous. I chose instead to help tidy our booth and keep an eye out. Reed would come to find me soon, I felt certain.

Melissa wasn't lying about the brochure display – it was toast. Most of the brochures were still in a box behind the stand though. Mindy placed some on the counter in the middle of our booth, fanning them out artistically.

Justin reappeared – I had completely forgotten about him.

'Felicity, I have been calling you. I just heard there was some kind of stampede in here.'

I pulled out my phone, checking the screen to discover there were eight missed calls, six of which were from Justin, plus a plethora of unanswered text messages. The button on the side had been knocked and my phone was set to silent.

'I'm sorry,' I shook my head. 'It's been kind of a crazy day.'

Justin was looking around, checking out the industry going on around us as our competitors and compatriots all finessed their displays back to as close to what they had been pre-debacle.

'I feel I may have missed a few things,' he commented.

Reed reappeared. He was making his way back to the event hall doors, checking each vendor as he went to get an update report.

We were about done getting our booth ready for the visitors, but if there were things to do, they could wait because I needed to grab a few moments with Reed. I caught his eye and got a nod in response.

He was coming to me.

To Justin, I said, 'I need you to meet, Philippe. He's a new hire.'

'New hire?' my master of ceremonies questioned. He offered his hand to Philippe, who gave it an effeminate shake.

'We haven't worked through all the ins and outs of it yet,' I explained. My current plan was to see if any of my friends in the makeup business needed someone. I knew I didn't.

Reed stuck his head through the side of my booth, making a big thing about nervously tapping the steel of its structure to see if doing so would kill him.

Then he mimed wiping his brow. 'Whew. You never know,' he joked with a smile. 'This looks back to normal,' he added, indicating my booth.

'We were lucky,' I agreed. He was looking at me, so saw when I twitched my eyes toward the back of my booth – I wanted him to come with me.

He came into the booth, but just as we both turned to go, aiming for the area behind the booth where we would be out of sight and could talk in private, Melissa turned up.

'Reed,' she called. 'You forgot your water.' She was holding his bottle, the same sports drink bottle I had seen him with every time so far. He never went anywhere without it.

And now the woman who wanted him dead was handing it to him.

'You should stay hydrated,' she advised. 'That's what you are always telling me, isn't it?' Her tone made it clear she expected him to quench his thirst right now.

Mindy, Philippe, and I were all staring at him, wondering what he might do. Surely he understood that she must have poisoned it.

I watched in mute horror as he popped the lid up.

'Thanks, Mel,' he winked at her. 'I was wondering where I left it.'

My jaw dropped open as he lifted the plastic bottle to his lips, and just as he went to put the nozzle in his mouth, I lunged forward and slapped it away.

Reed reacted as if I had gone mad.

'What the heck, Mrs Philips?'

Melissa marched toward me.

'I will not tolerate my staff being assaulted or abused, Mrs Philips. Kindly explain yourself.'

Her proximity to me caused Mindy to get involved. As Melissa put herself between me and Reed, Mindy stormed across the booth.

Reed bent to pick up the water bottle and in doing so placed himself directly in Mindy's path. For a second, I thought it was a deliberate move to stop her before she could get to Melissa, but he made no attempt to delay her.

Arriving by my side, Mindy placed a warning hand on the killer's shoulder. It was no surprise to find it was her left hand because her dominant right hand was behind her back where it undoubtedly gripped the handle of whatever she had there.

176

'Let's all be calm now,' Mindy warned – she knew not to tip our hand yet. 'What's in the water bottle?' she asked.

Melissa shot her head to the side to frown at my niece.

'I should imagine it is water,' she snapped.

All this distracted me, and it was only when I heard Reed give a thankful gasp of refreshment, that I realised he'd picked the water bottle up and taken a swig.

How could he have been so stupid?

No one was speaking. Melissa had her body toward me, but her head cranked around to the side to see what we were looking at. My breaths were coming in lumps, but nothing was happening.

Reed seemed fine.

I allowed my heart to start beating again, but then I saw it.

Reed was looking down at his bottle and he had an uncertain expression on his face. He made a sucking sound, licking at his teeth and acting as if he had an odd taste he wanted to get rid of.

'Reed?' I questioned.

Mindy took her hand off Melissa's shoulder, she too was becoming concerned for the head of security. Spotting a can of Coke on the table, Reed snatched it up.

'Hey, man, that's mine,' complained Philippe.

Reed swigged, droplets of the dark liquid falling from his mouth and dribbling down his chin as he turned to look at me with panic in his eyes.

'What's happening?' asked Justin, picking up on everyone else's reaction.

'Reed?' asked Melissa. 'Reed, what is it, babe? Are you okay? Are you choking?'

His eyes were bugging out and his face was going red.

Mindy rushed to his side, so too Justin, both arriving in time to grab him as he keeled over.

I screamed for help, running to get to the struggling head of security.

'What? What's happening?' cried Melissa, her feet rooted to the floor.

Swinging around to face her, I screamed, 'What did you put in his bottle?'

Melissa's eyes jerked toward mine and she backed away a pace.

'What was it?' I repeated. 'It's no accident this time Melissa.'

'Was there something in the bottle? Check his airway!' shouted Justin.

Mindy had hold of Reed's hand, her fingers looking like he was crushing them in his grip. 'Oh, God!' she exclaimed.

At that moment, white foam began to leak from Reed's mouth and his eyes went still.

Mindy grabbed his throat, checking his carotid artery and crying out in anguish when she felt no pulse.

'He'd dead!' she sobbed.

Philippe squealed, both hands going to the sides of his face. 'Oh, my goodness. You killed him!'

More people were arriving at my booth, coming to see what the latest fuss might be about. I heard muttering that it was always my booth and that I must be cursed or something. Primrose was probably behind them, stirring things up and making unhelpful comments to remind my partner firms how badly things had gone for me recently.

I ignored it all to focus on Melissa.

Rising to my feet, I came at her. The mob around my booth were three deep and cutting off her escape.

'You killed him!' I raged, jabbing a finger at her. 'You couldn't stand that he was in love with someone else, so you killed him. I know it was you who rigged my booth to electrocute anyone who touched it.'

'What?' Melissa backed away but reaching the edge of the booth found she could go no farther. 'I don't know what you are talking about,' she lied.

'You called Reed to come to my booth knowing he would try to save whoever got shocked first and when that failed, you came in here last night to rig the lighting gantry to fall. Then you watched until he was in place and tried to kill him again.'

Murmurs of disbelief were rippling through the ever-growing crowd.

'No,' Melissa tried to deny what I knew to be true. 'No, I would never hurt Reed. I love him. I just want him to come back to me. The things that have happened were just terrible accidents.'

'Ha!' I spat. 'They were made to look like accidents, and you might have gotten away with it, but you got impatient and poisoned him right in front of us. We all saw it. You wanted him to have the bottle you filled with poison. Your fingerprints are all over it, Melissa.'

This was great. I felt like a real sleuth. The crowd were watching, hanging off my every word as I revealed the killer. There was nothing Melissa could do to deny it because she was as guilty as they come.

'Give me the bottle,' she demanded.

'What?'

She repeated herself, 'Give me the bottle. I didn't put anything in it.'

I shook my head. 'That's evidence now, Melissa.'

I spotted members of the security team. They were at the back of the crowd of wedding fayre vendors and trying to squeeze their way through. They had no idea what had just happened and got a rude shock when they saw Reed's body stretched out on the floor.

Silence reigned, Mindy and Justin slumping back onto their heels as they let Reed's arms go.

I might have caught the killer, but it was a hollow victory for Reed was dead and I had failed to stop it from happening.

All around us, the faces of the vendors were in shock. Another life had been taken and the wedding fayre seemed to be cursed.

Mindy took off her jacket and draped it over Reed's face and upper torso, hiding the man's sightless eyes so no one had to see them.

As hotel security, looking bewildered, moved in to restrain Melissa, I felt the crushing shock of Reed's death hit me. My body started to shake, and I crumbled. As massive sobs made my shoulders heave, Justin came to me.

Wrapped in his comforting embrace, I gave in to my emotions and bawled my eyes out.

The police would be coming, the wedding fayre was closed for the day, if not the whole weekend.

A man took over, I soon found out he was Reed's second in command, Miles Hopkirk. Tall and thin, he proved himself worthy of the position, doling out tasks and emptying the event hall.

Justin was good enough to fetch me a chair and lower me into it.

The hubbub of noise filling the hall a few minutes ago was gone, the huge void now echoey whenever anyone spoke or made a sound.

Reed's body was untouched, left where it was for the police and probably a medical examiner to inspect when they arrived. It would be a murder enquiry and would suck up some of my time as I attempted to explain my part in the events leading up to Reed's death.

My tears were under control again, but I was left with the shuddering aftereffects one always gets. I felt terrible. I didn't know Reed – we met for the first time yesterday, but I had liked him and his death, when I was fighting so hard to prevent it, was going to take a while to come to grips with.

My chair was turned away from his body, I didn't want to see it.

There were only a few people left in the event hall and all were clustered in my stand or around it. Justin chose to stay with me, so too Mindy, and though Philippe was urged to leave, I think he was worried about running into Henri and his cronies again. Other than the four of us, there were two members of the security team.

The other security guys were either with Melissa who, still protesting her innocence, had been taken away and secured in her office where they could hold her until the police arrived, or were indeed outside waiting for the police.

182

I was lost in my thoughts, questioning what I could have done differently, when I heard Philippe scream.

The banshee wail pierced through the fug of my brain like icy water poured directly down my back.

Twisting in shock to find the reason for his fearful cry, I screamed myself.

Reed's corpse was sitting up.

'Don't be alarmed,' he said, pulling Mindy's jacket from his face.

'Waaaaahhhh!' squealed Philippe, the sound of his terror fading into the distance as he put up what had to be an impressive time for the hundred-yard dash.

Reed pulled an 'Oops' face.

Mindy sniggered. 'That was great.'

I was heaving oxygen in and out of my lungs as I struggled to comprehend what was happening.

Philippe's wails trailed after him. 'Zombiez! Zombiez! The dead are coming back to life!'

He hit the doors to the hotel lobby going fast enough that any faster might have resulted in time travel.

And careened off them.

They were locked.

'Do you think he is all right?' asked Reed, letting Mindy give him a hand up.

Mindy chuckled, 'Compared to what?'

Reed nodded his head at the two security chaps, sending them to pick the startled, and now semiconscious, makeup artist off the floor. Turning to me, he bowed his head solemnly.

'My apologies, Mrs Philips. I had not intended to cause you such distress.'

All I could do was blink, 'What? How?' I mumbled. 'How are you alive? I saw foam coming from your mouth.'

'Ah, yes,' Reed looked about, picking up Philippe's abandoned Coke can. 'It's an old trick one can perform with soda and a breath mint. I saw what Melissa was trying to do. I'm still struggling to come to terms with how desperately she wants me dead.'

I wasn't the only one struggling to keep up.

'We saw you drink from the poisoned bottle,' Justin argued.

Reed knelt next to the bottle which, like his body until a moment ago, was left where it had fallen for the sake of preserving evidence. He pointed to it.

'The cap is closed. I mimed taking a drink and pretended to swallow. The plan came to me in a flash, but I needed someone to declare I was dead.'

'That was me,' chipped in Mindy gleefully. 'When Reed stumbled into me, he asked me to play along, and used the cover my body presented to get a mint from his pocket.'

I remembered the order of events now. 'He gagged, grabbed Philippe's Coke can, and fell to the floor once he'd taken a swig.'

'I kept the mint and the drink in my mouth,' Reed explained. 'The reaction is almost instant, but I had to hold my breath and hope no one else checked my pulse.'

'That's why I stayed so close,' said Mindy.

I sucked in a deep breath and let my shoulder's sag. It was hard to process. Reed was alive, we had the bottle of poison Melissa wanted him to drink and the police were coming. There were witnesses who would testify regarding Melissa's actions and with the police investigating perhaps they would also find evidence to prove she tampered with the lighting gantry. Or maybe she would confess.

Either way, it was done, and I would not spend the next few days, weeks, or months pondering Reed's death and how I could have prevented it.

I wanted to rage at Mindy for putting me through the last ten minutes, but I knew there had been no time for her to tell me what they were doing. Nor could she have said anything afterwards because there were people here and they needed to see my genuine grief to buy the lie.

I was exhausted. It was mid-afternoon and I needed a lie down.

Getting off the chair and using the edge of my stand to get back to upright, I tested my legs. They felt wobbly. All of me felt wobbly, but I could rest now and be glad it was all over.

The one disappointment I felt was that Primrose wasn't behind it all. She would be gunning for me over the handbag and poop incident, and I would need to watch my back.

'I'm going to my room,' I announced my intention to have a rest.

'I'll help you, Auntie,' offered Mindy.

I waved her off.

'I'm not an old woman, Mindy. I can manage to make it all the way back to my hotel room.' I showed her a smile. 'None of us can go very far until the police have taken statements. After that, you should take the rest of the day off and do whatever you want with it. The police can find me in my room where I will be waiting with the minibar poised until they are done with me.'

No one posed an argument, and I probably wouldn't have listened if they had.

The guards unlocked the event hall doors to let me out, and doing my best to look in control and unflustered by horrible murders and unexpected resurrections, I made my way to the elevator.

I was asleep when the expected knock on my door woke me.

## When is a Crime Scene not a Crime Scene?

Reed used water from the water cooler in Felicity's booth to clean the taste of mint-laced Coke from his mouth. It was an odd combination that seemed to coat his teeth.

As expected, they did not have to wait long for the first police officers to arrive. It was a pair in uniform, a man and a woman, swiftly followed by another pair of men.

The first pair assumed control of the situation. The senior among them, a woman, sent the second pair with one of Reed's security guys to find the suspect. Then, when she got into the event hall, and found things were not as expected, she radioed back to dispatch that they were at the scene, and that the reports of a murder were inaccurate.

Reed did his best to explain, showing them the water bottle Melissa handed him and explaining about the accidents over the past twenty-four hours.

'You say there was a woman investigating?' questioned the female officer, looking around.

'My aunt,' said Mindy, holding up her hand so the cop would know who had spoken. 'She's kind of an amateur sleuth.'

The officer, Constable Penny Mayfair, leaned her head to one side so she could speak quietly to her colleague.

'You'd better warn the guvnor. You know his thoughts on amateur sleuths.'

Her partner, Constable Tom Collins, grimaced a little but set off to intercept Detective Chief Inspector Randall Smith.

Unaware at that point that the murder had been faked, the pair of officers not in the event hall read Melissa her rights and cuffed her.

Outside in the street, Chief Inspector Smith arrived in his car, parking right in front of the doors because he wanted to, and he could.

'Did I understand your message correctly?' CI Smith enquired, hurrying up the steps to meet Constable Collins. 'The dead body isn't as dead as first reported?'

Collins gave a dutiful, 'No, sir. It's quite a confusing tale, sir. Um, it involves an amateur sleuth, sir.'

Chief Inspector Smith stopped dead in his tracks a foot from the hotel's door and glanced back at his car. Did it count as his case if he never went inside the building?

With his feet twitching, and his conscience fighting his heart, he asked, 'It's not my dad, is it? Tall man, nearly eighty, has an enormous German Shepherd at his side?'

Constable Collins gave the senior detective a confused look. 'Um, no, sir. I'm pretty sure they said it was a lady.'

CI Smith sagged and put a hand on the hotel's door as if he needed it to keep him upright.

'Okay. That's not so bad then.' To the best of his knowledge, Randall believed his dad was somewhere in the northern half of the country. Honestly, he'd lost track, and the old man moved about so much it would not have shocked him one bit to discover his father creating havoc here instead.

Pushing his way through the door, CI Smith made his way inside, leading the constable, who did his best to keep up.

188

'Where to then, man? Show me where they are,' demanded the chief inspector.

Exasperated, Constable Collins asked, 'Do you want to see the suspect or the victim first, sir?'

'You mean the victim who isn't a victim and the suspect who might have not done anything?' CI Smith corrected the young constable pedantically.

'Yessir.'

Randall Smith flipped a coin in his head.

'Let's see the supposed crime scene.'

The hotel security standing in front of the event hall doors, parted to let the cops through.

CI Smith had been winding up for the day. It was Saturday afternoon and already dark outside when the call to investigate a murder came through. It sounded like the sort of case he wanted to put his name to and had already called off a promising date so he could be the first on the scene. Now he wasn't so sure there was anything here other than some old woman with an overactive imagination.

If that proved to be the case, he would give her a polite, but well-deserved dressing down and attempt to salvage his evening. To speed things up, he sent Constable Collins to fetch the suspect.

'You want me to bring her to the crime scene, sir?'

'But it's not a crime scene, is it, Collins? You already told me the man faked being poisoned because he believed his wife was trying to kill him.

189

That being the case, the suspect isn't suspected of anything. If she is in cuffs, please have them removed.'

Collins didn't move instantly. This was about as abnormal as things got. Well, apart from some really weird tales his mate in Rochester kept telling him about. There was some paranormal investigation agency down there and they ran into the strangest cases in the country. The local police, which his mate from the academy was part of, got called in to mop things up on a semi-regular basis.

'What are you waiting for, man?' asked the chief inspector, expecting the constable to hustle, not procrastinate.

'Um.' Unable to come up with a reason not to fetch the suspect – not one that he was willing to use on the chief inspector anyway, he said, 'Nothing, sir. Fetching the suspect now, sir.'

Shaking his head, CI Smith turned toward the expectant faces looking out from the first booth in the event hall.

'This was some kind of wedding fayre?' he guessed, speaking loudly so he would be heard. It was a way of getting people talking without asking them a question about what was going on.

A man in a suit answered, 'Yes,' and extended his hand, 'Reed Cartwright, head of security here at the Randecaux. The bottle containing the poison is over here.'

'How do you know it is poison?' CI Smith asked.

It proved to not only be a pertinent question but also a stumbling block for the security chief. Until that moment, he hadn't thought to question it.

'What else would it be?' enquired Mindy, her tone suggesting the contents of the bottle were obvious to all but a complete idiot. 'Melissa has been trying to kill Reed all weekend by staging accidents. This was just the latest attempt.'

'Poisoning someone hardly seems like it can be passed off as an accident,' remarked the chief inspector.

'She was getting frustrated?' suggested Mindy, in the impatient/bored tone only a teenager can muster.

CI Smith chose not to argue. He looked about at the assembled persons and waited for the supposed crazy murderer to arrive.

Buster exploded in a fit of barking, leaping from my bed – which I had to help him get onto in the first place – to attack the door. He was still wearing his cape, insisting he needed to keep it on because, *'Danger never sleeps'* as he put it.

He jumped at the door, misjudged his leap and slammed into the wood with his skull.

*'Dear Lord,'* muttered Amber.

Not wanting my pets to bother the police officers, or fire questions at me I wouldn't be able to answer while the police were with me, I hooked Amber under my arm and carried her to the bathroom.

'Come along, Buster,' I shooed him in the same direction and over my shoulder, shouted, 'Won't be a minute.'

*'But there might be danger outside,'* protested my Bulldog.

'It will be the police, Buster, I assured him. 'I need to give a statement. They might want me to go somewhere with them. If I am going to leave the hotel, I will make sure Mindy is with you before I go.' I shooed him the rest of the way and shut the bathroom door.

Amber had climbed onto the top of the cistern where the dog couldn't get her. They would be safe enough to leave for a few minutes.

Making sure I hadn't smooshed my hair too much by checking in the mirror by the door, I found sleep lines from the pillow on the side of my face. I rubbed at them, but the persistent little blighters wouldn't shift.

Giving up, I opened the door expecting to find a police officer or officers outside and couldn't hide my surprise to find Jessica looking back at me.

'Is everything all right?' I asked.

'Can I come in,' she begged. 'It's about Melissa Cartwright. I need to tell someone and I'm not sure who I should trust.'

Startled, I backed away from the door. Did she have the vital piece of evidence to prove Melissa was behind the accidents? Had she seen her cutting the cable from my refrigerator? I remembered Jessica was in my booth right around that time.

'Come in,' I beckoned.

Melissa's arrival back in the event hall caused a minor ruckus.

'What is she doing here?' Reed demanded the chief inspector explain.

When Melissa saw her husband standing, breathing, and talking, she fainted on the spot.

Chief Inspector Smith watched her collapse and blew out a frustrated breath.

'Yes. I suppose you are going to tell me that she was not made aware her husband's death was a ruse.'

The two constables who had been with her for the last ten minutes looked inward at each other. Sensing they were about to start blaming one another, CI Smith cut them off.

'Never mind.' He pointed a finger at Constable Penny Mayfair. 'Use an evidence bag to pick up that water bottle and bring it to me, please?'

'Sir?'

His evening was ticking away. The longer he spent here, the less likely it was he could rearrange his date.

'Come along. It won't bite. Wait, cancel that, I'll do it myself.'

## Not What I Thought

As Jessica came into my room, I poked my head through the doorway to check up and down the corridor. I was checking to see if the police were there – if Jessica had a big secret to reveal, they would want to hear it. There was no one in sight, so I ducked back into my room and closed the door behind me.

She had taken up a position across the room, fiddling with her handbag and I questioned if she had used her phone to take a photograph or a video of Melissa doing something criminal.

I started toward my bathroom door, intending to let the animals out again now there was no need to keep them in there, but stopped when Jessica took her hand back out of her handbag.

It wasn't her phone she'd been looking for. It was a knife.

A really big, dangerous looking kitchen knife.

Above the knife, Jessica's pleasant smile was now an angry sneer.

To say the change in attitude threw me would fail to capture how terrified and baffled I now felt.

'What's going on?' I gasped, backing away.

She took a step toward me, bringing the knife upward as a threat.

'Where is Reed?' she growled.

My eyes flared, and I almost blurted the truth, but I managed to catch myself. Jessica had been in the event hall with everyone else and had seen his act. So far as she knew, Reed was dead, so why was she now here asking me where he was?'

'He's dead, Jessica,' I replied as boldly as I could. My eyes were on her knife. Until she screamed her reply at me they were anyway.

'Liar!' My head snapped up to see the madness in her eyes and any question that Melissa might be the one behind the accidents faded away. 'I know he's alive. I know,' she repeated, advancing another step.

My feet moved without me needing to instruct them, fear making me back away, but my back hit the wall and I could go no farther. I was on the far side of the room, away from the door and my chance of escape. To get there I would have to go over the bed and the likelihood of making it before the madwoman caught me was slim to say the least.

'It was you,' I stammered, trying to work out what connection Jessica had to Reed and why she was the one behind the accidents. I wanted to ask why, but a different question surfaced. 'How do you know?'

Jessica's top lip curled back. 'How do I know he faked his death? He told my sister.' Her answer just added more confusion.

'Your sister?' I had no idea who she was talking about or why Reed might feel a need to make sure she knew he was still alive.

'Yes, my sister! The one he is trying to steal away from me! Well, I'm not going to let it happen, do you hear me?' Jessica was shouting. 'He thinks he can look after her better than me.'

I was edging toward the bathroom door. Buster was in there. So too Amber though I doubted she would be much help. My Bulldog though, he spent his life pretending he was a superhero. He'd barked when Jessica knocked on the door, but since then hadn't made a noise. If I let him out, he would create a distraction at the very least.

There was a lamp on the nightstand just a few feet away. I knew it was there and tried not to look at it, fearing Jessica might guess what I was planning.

'Are you listening to me?' she shouted, twitching the knife again.

Jolted by the anger in her words, I blurted, 'Sorry. Yes, your sister. Reed is trying to steal her from you.' Like someone opening a window to let in the light, the answer appeared before me as plain as day. 'Kimberly,' I gasped the name, the mesmerising puzzle melting away. 'Your sister is Kimberly, and she is in love with Reed.'

It was the wrong thing to say.

'She's not in love!' Spittle flew from her lips. 'Reed has her confused. He stole her from me!'

Keeping her talking as I edged closer to the bathroom door, I asked, 'Why is that bad? Reed is quite nice if you get to know him. Maybe you should give him a chance.'

'No!' she shrieked. 'We are going back to Ireland. Both of us. Reed has to die, now tell me where he is or so help me I will gut you and find him myself!'

I shoved the bathroom door open, screaming, 'Devil Dog! It's hero time!'

Buster was right behind the door, catching it in the face as I threw it open. I heard the thump and his grunt of pain, but he was ready, poised to do what I needed of him.

I feared for what Jessica might do. The thought that she might stab him before I could grab the lamp and stop her made my legs weak, but as Buster exploded from the bathroom, I threw myself toward the bed.

'*Dun dun, Dah!*'

Buster's ridiculous battle cry reached my ears.

Jessica screamed in rage, brandishing the knife but unable to work out which of us to target.

Reaching for the lamp, I turned my head to look at Buster and was therefore watching when his front right paw caught on the edge of his cape. Like standing on a loose shoelace, the cape stopped moving, yanking his head down as inertia carried him onward. Unable to recover, he tripped, went into a forward roll, and came to land on his back at Jessica's feet.

Terrified to the point where I genuinely thought I might wet myself, I snatched the lamp in my left hand and started running with it. It wasn't much against a knife, but it was all I had, and I was committed now. Maybe if I could get close enough to throw it …

The cable, wired or plugged in behind the head of the bed, reached the maximum extent of its reach and stopped dead. Gripping it tightly, my entire right arm also stopped, destroying my forward momentum though my legs didn't get that message for another half second.

With my bottom half going forward and my top half abruptly stationary, I flipped and landed next to my dog at Jessica's feet.

'What the heck was that?' she snarled.

Buster was trying to get up, flailing his legs to flip back onto his paws. I shot out an arm to hold him still. Jessica had all the advantage now. If we tried anything, we were going to get stabbed.

'*Pathetic,*' meowled Amber as she sauntered out of the bathroom and jumped onto the bed.

'*Get her, cat!*' barked Buster, still held in place by my arm.

Amber arched her back and stretched. '*I hardly think so. Suicide missions are your thing, dog.*'

I could not condemn her for refusing to help, we were in a no-win situation.

Jessica stepped back a pace, putting some distance between us when she said, 'Get up. Try anything like that again and I *will* kill you.'

I did as she commanded, moving slowly and with caution so as not to make her think I was about to have a second attempt at overpowering her. I wasn't that foolish. I also hooked a hand through Buster's collar to keep him from doing anything brave and rash.

'Put that dog back in the bathroom,' Jessica commanded.

'And the cat?' I asked, wondering if I could pick Amber up and throw her at the knife-wielding insane woman. I couldn't throw Buster – I could barely lift him, but an unexpected cat to the face might do the trick.

Jessica's reply derailed that plan. 'No, the cat can stay. I like cats.'

'*See?*' sighed Amber. '*Cats are universally loved by everyone. Even crazed killers favour us over dogs.*'

I had to use force to get Buster into the bathroom and shut the door as he barked his unprintable response and threatened, yet again, to kill the cat when he got the chance.

'*Why don't you tell her the police are coming?*' asked Amber casually. Her attention was on a piece of fluff drifting in the air, a front paw half raised and ready to bat at it. '*Might that not give her cause to go elsewhere?*'

199

Why hadn't I thought of that? Because I am petrified beyond the capacity for logical thinking, that's why.

'The police are coming to question me,' I told Jessica.

'I don't believe you,' she spat. 'Stop stalling. Tell me where Reed is.'

'It's true,' I insisted, 'They need a statement from me because I've been involved in what has been happening. I thought it was them when you knocked on the door.'

A flash of doubt shot through Jessica's eyes.

'I don't know where Reed is.' The knife came up again and I spread my hands in surrender. 'Honestly. I left them in the event hall to wait for the police and came for a lie down. The last couple of days have been stressful. Reed might still be there, but he might have gone somewhere else.'

Her lip twitching with anger and irritation, she snapped, 'Call him then. Get him on the phone and make him come here.'

'I don't have his number.' I really didn't.

'Liar!' she yelled, not for the first time.

'My phone is in my handbag. It's over there on the desk.' I pointed, and Jessica shot her eyes across the room to see where I was looking.

'Don't try anything,' she warned. She had to take her eyes off me to root through my handbag, but I wasn't going to try anything, not after the last attempt failed so spectacularly.

I gave her the code to unlock my phone once she found it and let her scroll through my contacts and the recent texts and calls.

Throwing my phone down in angry disappointment, she sneered at me with a twisted smile.

'I guess I have no need for you then, do I?'

The ball of fear in my belly writhed, threatening to make me vomit. I glanced at the door but there was no way I could get to it before she got to me. I swung my head the other way, looking at the window. I was three floors up which had to mean it was fifty feet or more to the ground outside which was pavement on this side of the hotel.

Could I survive that?

I thought I stood more chance with gravity than I did against Miss Stabby and her knife, but would the window even break if I threw myself against it? In a film it would, but this is real life.

'It's nothing personal,' she told me, making it almost sound like an apology as she hefted the knife and moved in for the kill.

I screamed and turned to run. The bathroom wouldn't offer me much protection – Jessica is bigger, younger, and stronger than me. Even if I got inside and managed to shut the door, she would be able to kick the door in. Or would threaten to kill Amber and I wouldn't be able to hide in fear while she did it.

Amber could probably do exactly that if the roles were reversed, but I couldn't.

My right foot came down, and my left was leaving the floor as I threw myself across the room to the one place of possible refuge and it was at that moment that the door to my room exploded inward.

## Figuring it Out

The door smashed against the wall with a thunderous crack but in that half heartbeat between the lock bursting and the door hitting its stop point, cops were streaming into the room.

Jessica shrieked like a madwoman, her voice competing against the bellowed orders coming from the police officers.

Unable to take my eyes from the men and women pouring through my hotel door, and still in full flight mode to get to safety, I lost my footing and fell to the carpet. With my view obscured by the bed, I missed what happened next and had to judge what was going on by the sounds I could hear.

Mindy appeared, leaping over the bed to find me.

'Auntie! Auntie, are you okay?'

'I'm in one piece,' I replied, certain I was a long way from okay.

She helped me to my feet, and I got to see Jessica being hauled off the floor. She was in cuffs, her hands behind her back and the knife was lying on the carpet. No one appeared to be leaking any vital fluids which allowed me to breathe a sigh of relief.

'*What's going on?*' barked Buster. '*Can someone let me out?*'

Still sitting on the bed, Amber sighed. '*All that danger and mayhem and the stupid dog survived again.*'

I asked Mindy to get Buster's lead and let my dog out. He was super excited to see so many new people and needed to be restrained.

'Mrs Philips?' enquired a man in his forties. He was wearing a sharp suit and was obviously the senior police officer in attendance.

I nodded. 'Yes. Thank you for coming to my rescue.'

'No need to thank me, Mrs Philips, I was not the one who cracked this case. I just happened to be here.'

Blinking in my confusion, I asked, 'So who was it?'

Mindy provided the answer. 'Reed and Melissa mostly, Auntie.'

'Yeah, they were like totally badass together,' added Philippe in his usual excited manner.

'Melissa?' I repeated her name automatically, only after I had said it did I acknowledge that if Jessica was the psycho killer, then Melissa had to be innocent.

The cops bundled the still-struggling Jessica out of my room and when they cleared the doorway, two more people filled it – Reed and Melissa.

I shot Melissa an apologetic smile. 'Sorry.'

She waved it away, hooking a thumb at Reed. 'He's the one doing the grovelling, Mrs Philips.'

'But how did you figure it out?' I begged to be told.

While I was upstairs asleep on my bed with Amber and Buster, the chief inspector had questioned the likelihood that Reed's bottle contained anything other than water. Melissa swore she hadn't done anything to it, so for the sake of expediency, he poured a small amount into a cup.

It looked like water, it smelled like water, and when he tentatively put his finger in it, it even felt like water.

Because it was.

Chief Inspector Smith had been ready to hand out a warning for wasting police time when Melissa insisted that there might be something to the suggestion the accidents were, in fact, staged.

It led them to look at all the vendors attending the event. It was the first time Reed had been given cause to check the list of names and he needed only about half a second to spot the one name that stood out - Jessica Bishop.

'Kimberly's sister,' I remarked.

Reed frowned. 'Why would you think they were sisters?'

It was my turn to frown. 'It's what Jessica said. It's her whole reason for wanting you dead. Jessica believes she is losing her sister to you because she is going back to Ireland and wants Kimberly to go with her.'

Reed shook his head. 'Jessica is an old flatmate of Kimberly's. Kimberly doesn't have a sister and isn't even Irish. I can believe that is what Jessica told you though. Kimberly moved out of Jessica's apartment months ago when Jessica started getting possessive.'

'Of Kimberly?' I questioned, wanting to make sure I was following correctly.

Reed nodded. 'Jessica changed her hair colour and style to look just like Kimberly and bought the same clothes she saw Kimberly wearing. She was truly nuts. When I met Kim, Jessica showed up here one day and threatened to kill me if I didn't end things. I dismissed it as nonsense but when I told Kimberly, she moved out of Jessica's flat, and we moved in together.'

'That's right, you did,' remarked Melissa coolly.

Reed chose not to react to his wife's comment. 'I thought Jessica had given up. It's been ages since Kimberly heard from her.'

'But here she is,' concluded Melissa, 'trying to kill you and wrecking my wedding fayre in the process.'

'It's not your wedding fayre, Mel,' argued Reed in a tired tone. 'It's the hotel's wedding fayre.'

'Which I organised, and your need for a younger woman destroyed.'

As the two fell to bickering, I slumped onto the edge of the bed.

Jessica must have found a job with a firm coming to the wedding fayre just so she could target Reed. It was why she slipped away when Reed came near earlier. She must have spotted him coming and knew he would recognise her.

Mindy explained that Reed put out a call on his radio, tasking the hotel security with finding Jessica, and gave them a description. In response, someone told him there was a disturbance on the third floor and they were heading there to investigate it. When they said the room number, Mindy knew it was mine. When she started running, they all went with her.

My survival was nothing more than blind luck.

I was right that the accidents were clever attempts to murder someone. I even identified who the intended victim was. About everything else, everything that mattered, I had been wrong.

Some sleuth I was.

The chief inspector moved into my eyeline.

When I looked up at him, he handed me a card.

'Mrs Philips, I will need a statement from you. It does not have to be today, but I must ask that you call this number,' he indicated a line on the card, 'in the next twenty-four hours to arrange to visit the station.'

I told him I understood and promised to do so.

He said a few more words before leaving, pushing Melissa and Reed out of my room just as a maintenance guy turned up to fix my door.

I was tired, emotionally exhausted, and the burst of terrified adrenalin had now drained away to leave me feeling spent.

The case was solved though I hadn't done much to solve it. In the morning, we would get one final chance to sell our business to the future brides and grooms visiting the wedding fayre. I didn't feel much like bothering, truth be told, and had it not been for the fact that Primrose would have free reign over everyone visiting if I wasn't there, I might have just gone home.

As it was, I picked myself up, sent Mindy and Philippe to get dinner and relax for the evening, and once I had changed my clothes and tidied myself up, I went to see a certain injured private investigator in the hospital.

Catching Fish

The final day of the wedding fayre went without a hitch. Melissa saw to it that everything the vendors and the visitors needed was there when they needed it.

Philippe arrived for work in a suit. Okay, so it was a zebra-print suit with a faux snakeskin collar that matched his cowboy boots, but it was a suit, and he even wore a tie.

Mindy had him handing out champagne and performing minor tasks. He seemed content to help where he could and proved to be both efficient and hardworking.

Henri came past my booth more than once, a scowl on his face each time. He made no attempt to speak to Philippe, or any of the rest of us, but I was left with the impression that we had not seen the last of him.

Late in the afternoon, Justin called me to meet a pair of clients he had at his table. They had been with him for almost an hour, going through their wedding needs and checking we could achieve all that they desired.

We could, obviously.

I gave them my best smile and thanked them for entrusting us with their nuptials, but meeting the woman who would helm their wedding wasn't Justin's reason for calling me over.

'They came here to meet Primrose Green,' Justin revealed.

Curious why he wanted to give me that snippet of detail, I saw the look the couple gave each other at the mention of Primrose's name. The man rolled his eyes.

'What is it?' I begged to know, desperate to hear juicy gossip about my awful rival.

Justin smiled knowingly when he said, 'She is a little overbooked.'

'She had no time to talk to us,' the woman explained.

Her fiancé picked up where she left off. 'Mrs Green has so many people in her booth, she cannot give any of them more than a few minutes. We even arranged an appointment to see her here more than two weeks ago.'

I smiled like the Cheshire Cat. That was Primrose all over. Gloss and glitter and shiny things to lure all the fish into her net, but the net had holes in it, and the savvy fish swam away again before she could land them.

I used a smaller net.

Mindy, Justin, and I dazzled the potential clients coming through the doors, winning them over by being good at what we do. We took twelve orders in one day, the single most successful day I have ever had at the event and when it was done, we collapsed into the chairs.

My feet hurt from being in heels. My back hurt from spending a good portion of the day standing up, but nothing was going to scare away my smile.

We had weddings lined up for the next year and beyond. Tomorrow we were all having a day off. It was a Monday, and we ought to be in the office, but our diary was quite deliberately devoid of appointments. We might miss out on some passing traffic because we were closed when people expected us to be open, but we needed a day off.

I needed a day off, that was for sure.

It was not unusual for me to work late at the office. I didn't have children or a husband to get home to, Buster was in the office with me, and Amber couldn't care less what time I got home provided I fed her when I arrived.

It was full dark outside - the sun had set hours ago at this time of year. I was beginning to get hungry and would leave the office soon, but I was trying to nail down the final table seating arrangement for a wedding in less than a month.

With over four hundred guests crammed into a ballroom it was not only a squeeze to get them all in, but the bride and groom (I suspected it was the groom's mother) could or would not agree on who was to sit closest to them.

This had been going on for weeks.

It might sound like a chore, and I guess it is, but it is also why I get paid the big bucks.

Mindy and Justin, the only two full-time members of my team who come to the office most days, had left more than an hour ago, both having stayed late to work on their parts of the many weddings we had booked.

Philippe, in case you are wondering, was working part time as we adjusted to having another member of the team. He wasn't local but lived within driving distance so for now he was commuting each day. I had expected to palm him off to one of my acquaintances in the makeup industry, but Philippe insisted he wanted to try something new.

Basically, I now had two assistants. Under different circumstances, that would be more than I needed, but with the royal wedding coming and the possibility that I might win the right to plan it, an extra pair of hands might prove of great value.

When I first heard the sound that evening, I thought it was Buster venting gas to atmosphere right next to my desk.

'Buster!' I complained.

My sleepy Bulldog lifted his head. *'Huh, what?'*

'Go over by the door,' I insisted.

He complied, well aware he was almost always the guilty party when it came to identifying the source of any unpleasant smells.

However, the sound came again, and this time it could not have been him. Not only that, now that I had heard it twice, it no longer sounded like escaping gas at all.

It was … it was more like a mournful moan.

I took my eyes away from my computer screen and listened. Nothing happened. Until I looked back down, that is.

Hearing it yet again, I got a rough sense of direction, and frowning, I got to my feet. It was coming from the stairs. Or, more accurately, it was coming from upstairs.

My office/boutique, at the bridge end of Rochester High Street, is in an old building erected long before electricity and indoor plumbing. It was the perfect place in a great location and clients could tell they had picked the right wedding planner just by standing outside and looking at my premises.

I climbed the stairs slowly, listening out for the sound again. They are old, wooden, and creak whenever anyone goes near them. In the quiet building, all I could hear were the creaking stairs so I hurried to the next floor, stopping just in time to hear the noise again.

The mournful moan, almost a sigh on the breeze had there been one, sounded like a voice. More specifically, it sounded like a child's voice.

I turned left, crossing the small landing to enter the room at the back of the house. It would have been a bedroom once and I knew – because the real estate agent showed me when I bought the place – that there were initials carved into the brickwork at the back of the fireplace.

The real estate agent had done some research, or was making it up quite convincingly on the spot, and had regaled me with the history of the building, its past uses and some of the families who had lived in it.

The initials belonged to three children living in the house more than a hundred and fifty years ago.

I used the room for storage. There were boxes of brochures and promotional material on the floor and box files of accounts stacked along one wall.

Imagine my horror when the almost voice came again, but this time I heard not the same mournful moan but words.

'Get out,' it demanded of me, sending a chill from the back of my head all the way down to my feet.

Five minutes later, crossing Rochester bridge in my car and still completely freaked out, I called Mindy.

'Auntie, what's up?' she mumbled around whatever she was eating.

My heartrate was slowing down but I had to take a breath to steady my nerves before I answered.

'Have you ever heard a noise coming from the upstairs storeroom?'

'A noise?' Mindy repeated. 'What sort of noise?'

'Um, like a ghostly wail?'

I heard Mindy jolt at the other end, I suddenly had her attention.

'We have a ghost? That is so cool.'

'I didn't say that.' I argued. I don't believe in ghosts, but I hadn't imagined what I heard.

'Don't worry, Auntie, I know just who to call.'

'The Ghostbusters?' I questioned, worried she was making a joke.

She laughed at the other end of the line. 'No, Auntie. There is a paranormal investigation agency just up the High Street from us. Have you never noticed?'

The End

## Author Notes

Hello, dear reader,

Thank you for getting to the end of this book, unless of course it is my mother reading this because apparently, she reads this bit first. Quite why I have no idea.

As you will have gathered in the last few words of the previous page, there is a crossover story coming. To be clear on that, the next book in this series will not be a supernatural adventure starring Felicity and crew alongside the Blue Moon team, but Tempest and his cohort will feature in a subplot occurring alongside the main story.

Did you know the collective noun for a group of swans is a bevy? I certainly didn't but the moment I wrote the word 'pack', I knew it had to be wrong. It's always fun to learn something. Now, I wonder what the collective noun for a gaggle of murder mystery authors is?

It is raining today in my corner of the world. I am in my log cabin as usual looking out over my garden. I need to mow the lawn, but it never seems to stop raining for long enough to let the grass dry out. Soon the grass will be too long to ignore and my fifteen-month-old daughter, Hermione, is already tripping on it.

Though it is August, and the sun is bound to return soon, the evenings are already starting to draw in and the air is taking on that familiar feel of autumn. My vegetable plots have been harvested – I need to get better at sowing succession crops – and the summer flowers have faded. Soon the leaves will start to change colour but before we get to that, I have a holiday planned.

It is a modest thing this year, a trip to Cornwall. My wife and I go most years, missing out in 2020 along with the rest of the world as we hid in our house and tried to avoid the deadly plague.

A few years ago, standing in a rockpool and holding my son's tiny hand, I conceived the idea for a book. It was right at the start of my author career but remains one of my favourite tales.

Will this year's trip inspire something new? The answer is probably. My head pops out ideas with alarming regularity, forcing me to pick which ones I will develop into books.

I mention whoopass in this book, specifically a can of it getting opened. If you are not familiar with this slang term, I will admit it is not one I have heard for a while, yet it was in frequent use not so long ago.

Intended as a jocular threat of violence, someone opening a can of whoopass intends to lay down a beating. It is the sort of hyperbole one might expect to hear from one of those overly muscular wrestlers on TV.

The rain has finally stopped, and this Englishman is in need of a cup of tea. I shall bid you all a good day and leave you with a promise that I will be starting to write my next book, A Shadow in the Mine, tomorrow.

Take care.

Steve Higgs

When Felicity Philips visits a wedding dress boutique only to find the designer strangled with one of her own veils, she finds herself unwittingly embroiled in yet another desperate investigation.

What could possibly be the motive behind the crime?

A single wedding dress is missing. A one-off design encrusted with jewels, it has been sold to three different brides, all of whom claim the deposit they paid makes it theirs. But who has it?

Find the dress and you find the killer.

Two of the brides are hers – she sent them to the designer!

With arch-rival, Primrose Green, stirring things up and the palace decision on who will run the next royal wedding looming, Felicity employs local P.I. Vince Slater to help solve the case, that's if he can keep his mind on the job and stop trying to romance her knickers off.

Can she uncover who wanted the dress badly enough to kill for it? She had better pray she does, because this is a dress to die for, and the killing might not be finished yet.

**Marriage? It can be absolute murder.**

There is no catch. There is no cost. You won't even be asked for an email address. I have a FREE Rex and Albert short story for you to read simply because I think it is fun and you deserve a cherry on top. If you have not yet already indulged, please click the picture below and read the fun short story about Rex and Albert, a ring, and a Hellcat.

When a former police dog knows the cat is guilty, what must he do to prove his case to the human he lives with?

His human is missing a ring. The dog knows the cat is guilty. Is the cat smarter than the pair of them?

A home invader. A thief. A cat. Is that one being or three? The dog knows but can he make his human listen?

There is no catch. There is no cost. You won't even be asked for an email address. I have a FREE Amber and Buster short story for you to read simply because I think it is fun and you deserve a cherry on top. If you have not yet already indulged, please click the picture above and read the fun short story about a dog who wants to be a superhero, and the cat who knows the dog is an idiot.

When a climber suspiciously falls to his death and a local artist has her dog stolen, both cases fall into the lap of local sleuth, Patricia Fisher ...

... but they should have come with a warning.

No sooner does she start to investigate, than a mysterious underworld figure issues a confusing threat. What has she uncovered?

Local boy, Sam Chalk, wants to help, his antics amusing but seemingly nothing more than a distraction. Does he know something though?

With time running out to save the dog, and the climber's death looking like nothing more than a terrible accident, a chance discovery will rock Patricia's world.

If only she had listened to Sam.

**Tempest Michaels is about to have a bad week.**

When a newspaper ad typo sends all manner of daft paranormal enquiries his way, P.I. Tempest Michaels has no sense of the trouble and danger heading his way.

In no time at all, he has multiple cases to investigate, but it's all ridiculous nonsense like minor celebrity Richard Claythorn, who believes he is being stalked by a werewolf and a shopkeeper in a nearby village with an invisible thief.

Solving these cases might be fun if his demanding mother (Why are there no grandchildren, Tempest?) didn't insist on going with him, but the simple case of celebrity stalking might not be all it seems when he catches a man lurking behind the client's property just in time to see him step into the moonlight and begin to transform.

All he wanted was a nice easy job where he got to be his own boss and could take his trusty Dachshunds to work. How much trouble can a typo cause?

**The paranormal? It's all nonsense, but proving it might get him killed.**

## More Books by Steve Higgs

**Blue Moon Investigations**

Paranormal Nonsense

The Phantom of Barker Mill

Amanda Harper Paranormal Detective

The Klowns of Kent

Dead Pirates of Cawsand

In the Doodoo With Voodoo

The Witches of East Malling

Crop Circles, Cows and Crazy Aliens

Whispers in the Rigging

Bloodlust Blonde – a short story

Paws of the Yeti

Under a Blue Moon – A Paranormal Detective Origin Story

Night Work

Lord Hale's Monster

The Herne Bay Howlers

Undead Incorporated

The Ghoul of Christmas Past

The Sandman

Jailhouse Golem

Shadow in the Mine

**Patricia Fisher Cruise Mysteries**

The Missing Sapphire of Zangrabar

The Kidnapped Bride

The Director's Cut

The Couple in Cabin 2124

Doctor Death

Murder on the Dancefloor

Mission for the Maharaja

A Sleuth and her Dachshund in Athens

The Maltese Parrot

No Place Like Home

## Patricia Fisher Mystery Adventures

What Sam Knew

Solstice Goat

Recipe for Murder

A Banshee and a Bookshop

Diamonds, Dinner Jackets, and Death

Frozen Vengeance

Mug Shot

The Godmother

Murder is an Artform

Wonderful Weddings and Deadly Divorces

Dangerous Creatures

## Patricia Fisher: Ship's Detective

Patricia Fisher: Ship's Detective

## Albert Smith Culinary Capers

Pork Pie Pandemonium

Bakewell Tart Bludgeoning

Stilton Slaughter

Bedfordshire Clanger Calamity

Death of a Yorkshire Pudding

Cumberland Sausage Shocker

Arbroath Smokie Slaying

Dundee Cake Dispatch

Lancashire Hotpot Peril

Blackpool Rock Bloodshed

**Felicity Philips Investigates**

To Love and to Perish

Tying the Noose

Aisle Kill Him

A Dress to Die for

**Real of False Gods**

Untethered magic

Unleashed Magic

Early Shift

Damaged but Powerful

Demon Bound

Familiar Territory

The Armour of God

Get sneak peaks, exclusive giveaways, behind the scenes content, and more. Plus, you'll be notified of Fan Pricing events when they occur and get exclusive offers from other authors because all UF writers are automatically friends.

Not only that, but you'll receive an exclusive FREE story staring Otto and Zachary and two free stories from the author's Blue Moon Investigations series.

## Yes, please! Sign me up for lots of FREE stuff and bargains!

Want to follow me and keep up with what I am doing?

Facebook